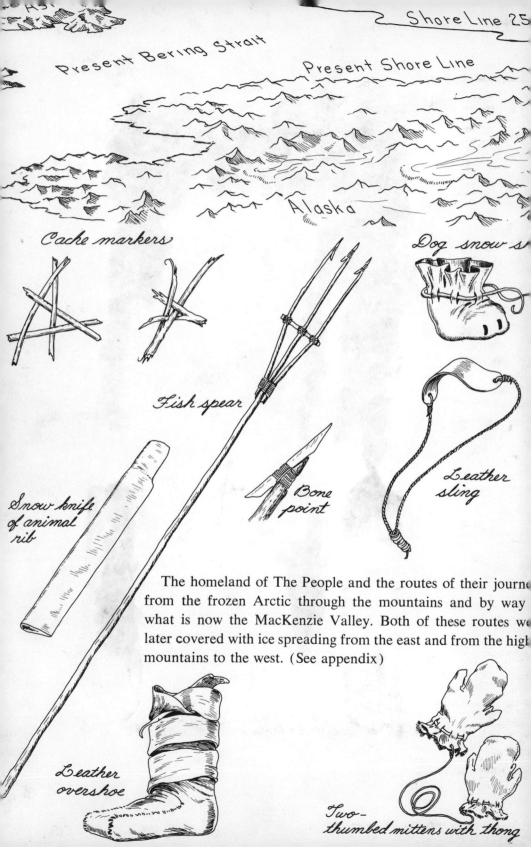

Present Bering Strait

Present Shore Line

Alaska

Cache markers

Dog snow s[...]

Fish spear

Snow knife of animal rib

Bone point

Leather sling

The homeland of The People and the routes of their journe[...] from the frozen Arctic through the mountains and by way [...] what is now the MacKenzie Valley. Both of these routes we[...] later covered with ice spreading from the east and from the high[...] mountains to the west. (See appendix)

Leather overshoe

Two-thumbed mittens with thong

THROW STONE
THE FIRST AMERICAN BOY
25,000 years ago

THE FIRST AMERICAN BOY
25,000 years ago

THROW STONE

E. B. SAYLES and
MARY ELLEN STEVENS

illustrations by Barton Wright

Reilly & Lee   Chicago   1960

for Myrta and Ray Fish

Authors' notes

THE STORY of Throw Stone takes place in a prehistoric period, 25,000 years ago. It is not "just a story" imagined by us. It is a historical reconstruction.

How the people lived 25,000 years ago can never be established exactly, but in recent years several scientific fields have come up with enough facts to piece together a picture of how it could have been.

There were two land routes by which people may have come to America from Asia (the Coastal route may have been the most difficult to follow, until people used boats—because of the many large rivers that had to be crossed). People may have lived along the shores of the Arctic Sea in Asia long before they came to America. As their numbers increased, and game became scarce due to the spread of the glacial ice, they would have sought new lands.

For the facts on which the story is based, the senior author has drawn on his forty years of archaeological experience and from the writings of others—which are acknowledged in the appendix.

From the background material gathered by the senior author, the junior author has woven the story. But each of us assumes responsibility for the "interpretations" that have been made of the source material. It is the way we think people lived in America 25,000 years ago.

What do you think?

E. B. SAYLES
MARY ELLEN STEVENS

THROW STONE
THE FIRST AMERICAN BOY
25,000 years ago

LAND OF ICE AND SNOW

*Two-piece bone fish hook
with shell lure and rawhide line*

THE BOY called Throw Stone and his grandfather walked far out
on the frozen sea. They walked to where a fishing stick—frozen
fast in the ice—pointed to the sky. The boy grasped the stick and
tried to move it.

"See, Grandfather? Our fishing hole is solid with ice like the
rest of the sea. We shall never catch another fish."

The Grandfather, too, tried to move the stick. He shook his
head sadly. "First no animals, now no fish."

Throw Stone smiled. The boy had a mouth full of big white
teeth and he could usually bring a laugh by showing them. But
the Grandfather looked away. His face was like a raven's: peaked
and sharp.

1

Covered from head to toe in fur clothing, with only wind-brown faces and hands showing, the two walked toward a rocky slope of rounded boulders and coarse dark sand. Their backs were to the gusty wind that struck the ice and drove the hard pellets of snow like drifting sand.

This had always been the warmest time; the beginning of the last summer moon when the sun never dipped entirely below the horizon. What had happened? During early summer when the ice had begun to melt, the Grandfather had smiled and said the hunting would be good. Then the evil wind came and froze the land and water; turning the summer back to winter.

The Grandfather raised his fist and shook it. "This is the work of the evil Acaba! First he made the animals go away and now, when the sun is in the sky, he has frozen the sea, so we cannot fish. He wants to see us starve!"

The boy trembled with fear. He looked at the dark red sun that hung over the vast grey waste of snow and ice. He thought of the tales his grandfather told; tales of Acaba who lived on the far side of a distant river; Acaba—the red cloud that cried out like the wind as it shrieked between the rocks along the beach. No animals, birds nor fish lived where Acaba was, for wherever he went he took with him cold winds to drive them all away. This was the story the boy had heard from his grandfather who, as a child, had heard it from a hunter who had traveled to the wide banks of Acaba's river.

Throw Stone and his grandfather climbed the rocky slope above the icy sea. The boy could hear the old man breathing hard.

"Look," said the Grandfather, pointing to a distant ridge. "Someone comes. Dark Hunter or Silent Tongue. Or perhaps a stranger."

Throw Stone nodded. "I wish it would be a stranger," he thought. "I wish it would be a stranger who had a son I could

2

play with." But it wouldn't be, of course. It was sure to be Dark Hunter or his brother, for theirs was the only other family left in the homeland.

"It can only be bad news," said the Grandfather. "Someone without meat, someone hurt. No longer does our homeland bring joy."

Throw Stone sighed. Everyone was hungry. And when people's stomachs hurt with hunger, nobody smiles.

They walked higher up the slope. Here, two mounds of earth, stones and driftwood were connected by a lower ridge. This was their home.

While they waited for the visitor, the Grandfather again told of the days before Acaba sent the cold winds. Then, when the sun was at its highest, the sea ice would melt and there would be many animals to hunt.

In the past, the caribou came to eat the moss that grew on the rocks or in the shallow dirt between them. Each summer, the low plants would find their way out from the cold ground to the sunlight only to be nipped back to the roots by the hungry animals. Seals came to the rocks on the shore; white bears stalked the seals; white foxes stole what they could from the bears; and black ravens ate the remains which no other animal would.

While the Grandfather talked, Throw Stone thought of how little food there was now. His father had killed two seals during the short time the ice was free from the shore but that had only been luck. The seals had come onto the rocky land, and before they could scramble back to sea, the Father speared them.

In the first moon of summer, when the ice was mushy the Father had jammed a heavy piece of driftwood into the frozen sea and had worked it back and forth to make a fishing hole. During the first two summer moons they moved the stick now and then to keep the hole from freezing solid. Sometimes they caught a fish but mostly they watched; waiting for the float fastened on

3

the sinew line to bob. But, now there was nothing even to watch. The hole had frozen as solid as the sea all around.

The visitor drew closer. He raised his hand in sign of friendship and the Grandfather returned his greeting. It was Dark Hunter. When he reached them, he thrust the shaft of his spear into the loose gravel covering the ground. "My family has only a few fish left," he said. "Summer will soon be over and the six cold moons of the dark winter will be upon us. The animals did not come this summer; none will come this winter. We will starve. You, Wise Hunter, tell us what we must do."

The old man's beady eyes glared at the red sun on the horizon. "The animals came to us from the south in summers past, then returned south in winter. Now our summer has turned to winter. We must go far to the south and find the animals. Our families must leave the homeland."

"But how do we know the animals are there!" cried Dark Hunter. "Perhaps when they left our land and went south, they disappeared into the mist. How can we know? No man has ever followed."

"When I was a boy," said the old man, rubbing at his sharp nose, "I heard stories of a land to the south where the sun lives. There are great dangers in reaching this land but it is there— with animals as far as the eye can see."

Dark Hunter took up his spear. "Then we will find it."

Throw Stone jumped around in front of the men. "We? You mean me, too? We are all going on a journey?"

The two older men ignored him, and the Grandfather motioned to Dark Hunter. "Come. We will talk with my son."

The Grandfather and Dark Hunter went to the smaller of the two mounds and lifted aside a hardened animal skin covering a small opening. They entered on hands and knees.

Throw Stone watched them disappear. Then he turned and walked toward a driftwood log to which three dogs were tied with

twisted lengths of hard skin. All three lay with their hind paws drawn under their bodies and their noses pressed into their fore-paws for warmth. The youngest of the three belonged to Throw Stone, and was called Yodi which means Happy Dog Which Likes Boy.

Like the other dogs, Yodi was dark brown with tan sides and looked like the foxes that came to the sea in summertime. He appeared big but was mostly bones under his soft fur, for he was fed only animal bones after the meat had been stripped from them. When he was not tied, he sometimes caught a rabbit or dug the mice from their hiding places.

Yodi whined and the boy knelt in the snow and patted him. Throw Stone still played with Yodi as he had when the dog was only a puppy and he still a child. But now that he'd learned a man's work, he knew his father scorned his playing with a grown dog. Dogs were kept only to carry loads. The other dogs, a big one called Dog That Bites and Old Dog, whose back was streaked with grey, snarled at the boy and drew away from him. Only his grandfather could touch Old Dog—who looked half frozen, with the snow on his eyelashes and whiskers.

"You're hungry, Yodi," said the boy. "But Grandfather says we're going to the Land Where the Sun Lives and there we'll find the animals. When we go to this new land, I promise to take you. You'll eat good red meat and grow fat." He smiled at the dog and Yodi showed his teeth in what looked like a smile.

Throw Stone laughed. "You have bigger teeth than I do!"

He left the dog and went to the mound that Dark Hunter and his grandfather had already entered. He crawled inside the small room and stood up on a floor covered with stalks of coarse grass. With a small bunch of stalks, he whipped the loose snow from his furs. On the opposite side of the room, an opening led into a dark passageway. On hands and knees, Throw Stone made his way through the passageway.

7

It led to a larger room, lit only by a burning wick in an oil-filled clamshell. Here were his father, his grandfather, Dark Hunter, his mother and his grandmother. Their black hair blended with the shadows cast by the dim light.

Throw Stone stood erect and removed his furs and skin boots. Now, clad only in skin trousers which came down to cover his feet, he was dressed like the others in the room. He joined them on the low skin-covered platform where they were seated.

The Grandfather took a piece of red meat, held one end of it in his teeth and cut a bite with an upward stroke of a stone flake. He then handed it to Dark Hunter who took a bite; it was passed on to the Father, then to the women and finally to Throw Stone who got only a very small piece. He chewed on it a long time to make it last, for his hunger was like a knot in the middle of his stomach.

The group talked long of the perils they faced with the coming of the long dark cold winter. There was not enough meat to live on until the next hunting time.

Finally the Grandfather said, "The decision is made. We will leave our homes and make new ones far away to the south where the animals live."

Throw Stone hugged his arms together. So it was really true— they were leaving!

THE HOME BY THE SEA

*Clam shell lamp with
grass wick and blubber*

THE GRANDFATHER hovered above them now, and the flame from
the clamshell lamp lit up his bird-like face.

"We will go to the Land Where the Sun Lives," he repeated,
then pointed to Dark Hunter. "We will divide the food between
the two families and set out in different directions. This way one
of the families may find the land of the animals, and The People
may survive.

Dark Hunter shook his head. "My family has no food to divide, only a few fish, and your family has seal meat and much
fish."

The Grandfather lifted his chin high. "You know the custom.
The food will be divided evenly."

Throw Stone looked around the familiar room. He thought of never again seeing the circular walls covered with animal skins. Never again was he to feel its coziness with the smell of fish, damp animal skins and warm bodies.

The Grandfather continued, "There are two ways to the land where the animals live. One is through the mountains. The other is by way of the valley beyond the homeland. The boy will draw straws to see which way each family goes."

Dark Hunter frowned. "Wait. What do we know of these two journeys? What do we know of animals or spirits that might kill us?"

The Grandmother leaned forward and her long grey hair fell forward, almost covering her wrinkled face with its flat nose. "I know a story of mountains. Listen."

She rocked back and forth, her loose-skinned arms locked across her bosom as she chanted softly:
"Far off in big mountains there is a river
A river full of moving water and jumping fish
The People walked in the moving water
And gathered the fish in their arms
While on the shore waited the brown bears
To kill The People and take their fish
Sometimes the brown bears walked in the water
And taller were they when they stood in the water
Than the white bears that live on the ice
And the brown bears were more than The People
So The People went away
And came to live by the cold sea
And this was long ago
Told to me by my grandmother
Who heard it from her father
It must be true
But it was long ago."

10

When Throw Stone heard this sad chant he moved closer to his father. The Father had killed many bears, and bore a wide jagged scar all the way across his face to prove it.

Dark Hunter said to the Grandfather, "You, Wise Hunter, do you know of the valley way?"

The Grandfather nodded. "I knew a hunter that went by way of the big valley. As I have told you often, the valley goes by the ice mountains. It leads to the land of Acaba, the red woolly spirit that sends cold winds to drive off the animals. Far, far away is the big river where Acaba lives. If The People overcome Acaba, they can go beyond to the Land Where the Sun Lives, where the animals are—" His voice trailed off. "Surely the animals are there."

The Father said, "How can we overcome Acaba?"

The old man closed his eyes. "I do not know, but one of us must not be afraid to fight when the time comes."

Throw Stone trembled. Even his wise grandfather did not know how to overcome Acaba!

"I hope we go by way of the mountains," he thought. "My father has killed many bears, but who could fight an evil spirit?"

The Grandfather lifted his gnarled hands before him. "The danger is great. But where the bears live, there live the fish. The People can kill the bears for their meat and catch the fish. And beyond where Acaba lives there are animals. The People must overcome Acaba. I have hunted long and am called Wise Hunter. When the animals do not come to us, we must go to them."

He broke a stem of coarse grass into one long and one short piece which he closed up in his fist. "This is the way The People have always chosen. The short one shall be by way of the mountains; the long one by way of the big valley. I do not know how long the journeys will be nor who will live or die."

The old man extended his wrinkled hand toward the boy. "My Grandson will draw first for Dark Hunter."

The stems lay hidden side by side except for two lengths that

11

barely could be grasped. Throw Stone licked his lips and extended his hand, hoping to draw the long straw for Dark Hunter so that Dark Hunter would go by way of the valley where Acaba lived. He pulled a straw free and his heart sank. It was the short one! Dark Hunter would go to the mountains and the boy's family through the valley to the land of Acaba.

Throw Stone covered his face with his hands, thinking of the evil one; the red cloud as big as a mountain. What would Acaba do to a boy who had never hunted alone; who had never helped to kill anything larger than a caribou?

Dark Hunter left, saying, "I will bring my family and belongings soon."

Throw Stone looked at his mother and his grandmother. He could see sadness in their faces for having to leave their home. But, he knew they would say nothing and do whatever the Grandfather and the Father told them. His mother was little more than a moving shadow who did the Father's bidding. Still, there were the times when she laughed and talked with the Grandmother and Dark Hunter's wife. To Throw Stone, she had always been a pair of comforting arms that reached out to soothe him. But now, he was too big to show he might like to be comforted.

Throw Stone also had to silently obey his father, so he fought back his own sadness at having to leave the only home he remembered. His grandfather had carried him here as a baby when the family had moved from a land which lay far to the west.

As if the Grandmother knew what he was thinking, she chanted the old song:
"Long ago The People lived along the shore of the sea
Many, many journeys away from where we now live
But there were too many mouths to feed
And the animals too few for all to hunt
Some of The People came to this home by the sea
Then no more of The People came

Where are the others now?

Oh, where are the ones we left behind?"

The Grandfather said to the boy and the Father, "We will prepare the hunting pouches and carrying bags." Then he turned. "Women, divide the meat."

Throw Stone sat on the platform filling his small hunting pouch; carefully wrapping his few bone points in soft skin. He watched the Grandmother and the Mother drag a skin bundle from the passageway into the circle of light cast by the oil lamp. From the bundle they took thin, narrow pieces of dried meat. They placed the meat in two piles, one on each of the raw skins that lay on the floor. Everything was evenly divided so that Dark Hunter's family would have half. Throw Stone looked at the meat hungrily. He longed to snatch a piece of it and run off, the way Yodi would do, if he had the chance.

Beside each pile of dried meat, the women added a small bit of animal fat in seal skin containers. From the passageway they next pulled the dark red carcass of a seal. It was frozen stiff. With their stone knives they hacked it into thick slabs and piled the hunks of meat in equal amounts alongside the other piles. Next, they dragged another bundle of skins from the darkest edge of the room and from it separated a pile of dried fish, each split from head to tail.

The Grandfather sat cross-legged on the fur-covered platform with his hunting pouch between his knees. His dark body was wet with perspiration. Against the wall were four spears of straight driftwood; three long and one short. The old man selected one of the long spears and held it in his hand for balance. From behind the platform he drew out a bone point and fitted it into the slotted end of the spear. Sinew was tightly wrapped around the wooden shaft where the bone point fitted into the spear.

He smiled at Throw Stone. "Never wrap the point and spear together," he explained. "For when an animal has been speared,

13

the point must pull free. If it does not, the animal will carry away your spear and you will be standing there to face the animal with nothing but your own fingers."

"I know this, Grandfather."

His grandfather chuckled. "Do you? I saw you spear a rabbit and the rabbit ran away with your spear."

Throw Stone tucked his head and laughed. It was true! He still made so many mistakes that he was not allowed to hunt alone.

The Grandfather selected six other bone points and wrapped them in skin for his hunting pouch. Then he put in the bone and stone tools he used for making the points. Last of all he added a small bag with tools for making fire.

The Father finished packing his hunting pouch and went to fetch their snowshoes from the room beyond the passageway.

"Grandfather," said Throw Stone. "I fear Acaba. I'm afraid he'll kill me. I've gone with the hunters to kill the seal, the walrus, the snow rabbit and the caribou, but how do I hunt the red cloud if I should see it?"

"You must have magic," the old man replied. From his hunting pouch he removed two small slender stones, bound together with sinew. The boy had long known the stones were his grandfather's greatest possession—his powerful, magic-working charm.

"This is now yours," the old man said.

"But Grandfather—what will you do without it?"

"My grandfather gave it to me," he said, then his eyes grew bright in his sharp face as he chanted in a high whine,

"When I was a boy, my grandfather gave the charm to me
For he had received it from his grandfather
I have carried it ever since
I am known as Wise Hunter but now I am old
I have killed many bears and I am not afraid
You, too, must not be afraid
The charm will do good or evil

14

Whatever you ask of it

Ask that you will be a great hunter."

Throw Stone ran his hands over the stones and closed his eyes. "Make me a great hunter." Then he opened his eyes and smiled broadly at his grandfather. The Grandfather laughed and patted him on the knee.

Throw Stone placed the charm in his hunting pouch. "I want to be a great hunter like you, Grandfather."

"Then keep the magic close to you," said the Grandfather, "Until the time comes when you can pass it on to your grandson. May it serve you as well as it has me and all our ancestors!"

Charm stones wrapped with sinew

THE JOURNEY BEGINS

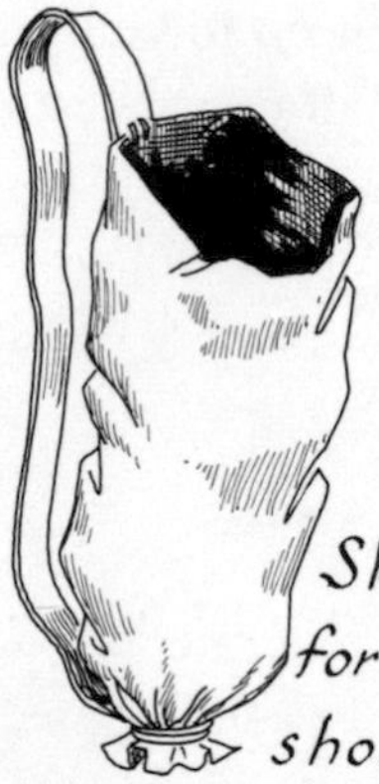

*Skin carrying bag
for men – on left
shoulder*

THE FATHER returned with snowshoes made of driftwood bound with thongs. The Father and boy stuffed them into long carrying bags of skin, along with extra spears, and a bundle of soft skins wrapped with thongs. In each carrying bag they placed a smaller skin bag that contained one of the piles of dry meat.

The Grandfather selected his best skin clothing for the long journey and spread it alongside the carrying bags, spears, and his sling.

"What's wrong with my grandfather?" wondered Throw Stone. "Why is there a high color in his face? Why are his actions quick like those of a young man?" Only the sleep before, he'd been

16

gasping and coughing and crying out that he was older than the sea. But now—why was he singing so much?

The Grandfather squatted, then hopped around the room like a song bird. Again he sang:

"This is the home where we lived happily together
Once the animals came with the warm wind
But Acaba drove away the warm wind
And now there are no animals to hunt
Once I was known as Wise Hunter
But now I am an old man
My life goes on in my son
And his life goes on in my grandson
If I go out and never return
My spirit will stay close to my grandson
He will reach the Land Where the Sun Lives
He will destroy Acaba, the evil spirit."

Throw Stone did not understand what his grandfather meant, but the Grandfather was very wise. If he believed the boy could destroy the evil spirit, perhaps he could, especially now that the Grandfather had given him the powerful charm!

The Grandfather came to him and put his arm across his shoulder. "Go to sleep," said the old man. "You must be strong for the long journey. Go to sleep. And I, too, will go to sleep."

Throw Stone crept under a bear skin and closed his eyes. Soon he heard the rest of the family crawling under the animal skins, settling down to sleep.

The howling dogs awoke Throw Stone. Clad only in his skin trousers and skin boots, he crept from beneath the furs, and walked toward the passageway. The dogs howled again, in a way that Throw Stone had never heard. It filled him with fear. He crawled through the passageway into the small room. The outside light lit one edge of the skin that covered the doorway. Pushing

17

the dry skin aside, Throw Stone was almost blinded by the whiteness of new fallen snow.

When his eyes grew accustomed to the brightness, he stepped outside. Now he saw why the dogs had howled. There were tracks on the ground; tracks of someone without skin boots that led away from the doorway. The tracks were easy to see near the shelter of the house mounds where the snow was thin on the bare rocks. Here the footprints had pressed through the snow and left only dampened outlines. He followed the tracks. They led to where the dogs were leashed, but now there was only Yodi and Dog That Bites. Old Dog was missing. Only his Grandfather could touch Old Dog! The dog's tracks joined the footprints as they went toward the rocky slope. Here the footprints were covered with snow. Throw Stone looked down the slope. It was as unmarked as the beach beyond.

He hurried back inside, hating to admit to himself that he knew who had gone away. He crawled through the passageway, shaking with cold, and afraid to look at his grandfather's sleeping place. It was empty. Near his own place was a pile of fur clothing, on top of which lay his grandfather's hunting pouch and best spear. The Grandfather had taken only his spear sling.

The Father watched Throw Stone return to the skin-covered platform. Throw Stone fought back his tears. "Why did he do it?"

"It is the custom," said the Father. "He did not want to be a burden when we made the journey through the valley. Old Dog could never be given to anyone else, so your grandfather took the dog with him. He also took his sling for that, too, can never be given to anyone else."

Throw Stone shook his head. "I still don't understand."

The Father touched his shoulder kindly. "If the old people did not go away to die when there is not enough food for all, the young ones could not live. The young must have enough food so they will be strong and can hunt. Remember, the most important thing of all is that The People survive."

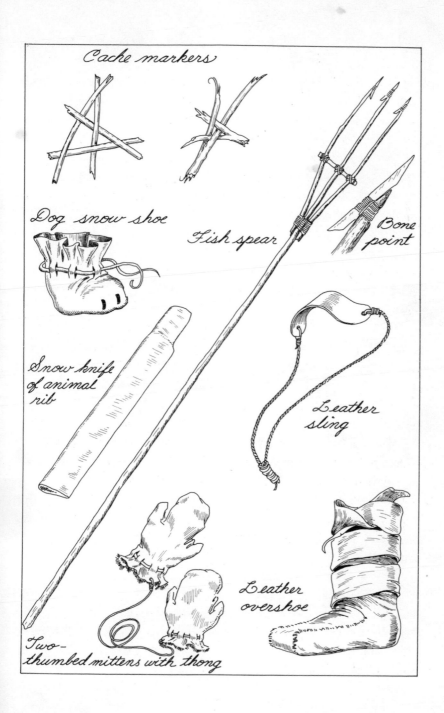

Cache markers

Dog snow shoe

Fish spear

Bone point

Snow knife of animal rib

Leather sling

Two-thumbed mittens with thong

Leather overshoe

"But where did my grandfather and Old Dog go?" asked Throw Stone.

"Together they walked far away from the house and lay down to sleep. They were not cold, for the sleep that lasts forever is rosy warm."

Now Throw Stone knew what the Grandfather had meant in the song. His spirit would go in the charm stone and help the boy against the evil Acaba.

Throw Stone stooped to touch the things his grandfather had left him. "Thank you, Grandfather," he whispered. "Thank you."

The others, also aroused by the howling dogs, were awake under their sleeping skins. The Grandmother in her low voice sang the mourning chant while the Mother covered her tear-streaked face with her hands. So they, too, knew that the Grandfather had gone away. Throw Stone's heart was heavy and he longed to join his mother in weeping, but he knew that his father expected him to act as a man. It was the custom that men should not show their grief, no matter how much they felt it.

The family gathered around the oil lamp. Throw Stone looked at his father who was now the head of the family. Decisions which had been made by the Grandfather must now be made by him.

"We will go on the journey as was decided," the Father said. "But the women will stay here until the new land is found. My son and I will go alone. I do not know if it is possible, but I hope to return for you, my mother and my wife, before the six cold winter moons have passed."

"And the dogs?" asked Throw Stone.

"They will be left here," the Father answered. "They will be needed to carry the skins later, after we have found the new land."

Throw Stone could endure no more. He thought of leaving his home, his mother, his grandmother, his dog—to face Acaba. He wanted to throw himself in his mother's arms and be comforted as he had when he was a child. But his father was watching him closely.

21

"We must be ready to leave when Dark Hunter comes," said the Father.

"But Yodi—"

"No," his father answered and turned from him. There was no use arguing. Yodi and Dog That Bites would come with the Mother and the Grandmother. They would carry the loads to the new home that he and the Father must first find.

While the sun was still high in the sky, Dark Hunter came with his brother and the women. The Brother was called Silent Tongue because he couldn't speak. On their backs, the men carried hunting pouches, snowshoes and mittens; in their hands each carried a hunting spear. Dark Hunter's wife and their daughter followed.

The Daughter was called Strong Girl because she had long been able to carry a woman's load. Across her forehead was a broad fur-covered strap which was fastened to a bundle of skins and clothing on her back. Below this was a skin bag for the meat and fish she would get from Throw Stone's family. She also carried snowshoes. Like her mother who carried a similar pack, she was bent forward so that she could see only the ground near her feet.

Throw Stone went to help her. When the carrying strap was lifted from her forehead, the heavy pack stood alone, for it was lashed together with narrow strips of fur skin. As Strong Girl looked up, Throw Stone turned away from her to kick at some gravel.

Dark Hunter and his family were told that the Grandfather had gone away with his dog. They, too, were sad. Wise Hunter had long been respected by all The People. The older women mourned together as the men went about their preparations for the journeys.

Strong Girl stood to one side, staring at the boy. He showed her his grandfather's hunting pouch, opened it and when she saw the charm stone, she drew back. He quickly covered it up. He allowed her to touch the small bag with the fire stones and moss.

"Can you make fire, Throw Stone?"

22

He closed the bag. "Of course." But he wasn't sure he could, although he'd watched it done many times.

"If you were a boy," he told her, "then you could be a hunter like me."

Strong Girl tossed back her long dark hair. "I don't want to be a hunter." She walked off to join her mother.

When the meat and fish were packed in the women's bags, Dark Hunter and the Father touched each other's arms.

Dark Hunter said, "May you escape Acaba, the evil one, and reach the Land Where the Sun Lives."

The Father replied, "May you overcome the brown bears and may our two families meet again."

Dark Hunter and Silent Tongue helped the women into their bundlesome packs again. The family departed with the two men walking ahead.

Throw Stone knew he, too, would soon be leaving. He ran to his dog and patted him.

"I promised to take you with me, Yodi, but I can't. My mother will bring you to me later." The dog whined and wagged his bushy tail.

The boy watched Dark Hunter's family as the four trudged over a slope and disappeared. The dark rocky land was bare of snow except where the wind had banked it. Far to one side, the sun was a rose-colored disc in the grey sky that joined the ice sea.

His father called to him. "Get your pack. We must start our journey."

SLEEP WITHOUT FIRE

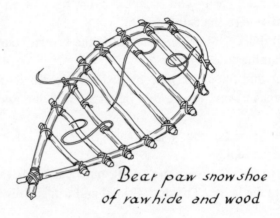

Bear paw snowshoe
of rawhide and wood

NEITHER Throw Stone nor the Father looked back. The boy knew the two women were watching as they walked beyond the farthest hill and down the last slope where they could be seen.

Here, in the summers before, the Father, Dark Hunter, Silent Tongue and the boy used to return from the hunt. In those times, that seemed so long ago, the women back at the home strained their eyes to catch the first glimpse of them. They would know if the hunt had been a good one by the way the men were walking under their loads of meat. On the hilltop they just had passed, the women used to meet them and help carry the heavy loads home.

The bare stony slope of the hill danced with puffs of dirty

snow, but the strong, cold wind had died down. This was the land where once the animals had come in great herds. They had come when the sun was in the sky as it was now; the time of the last summer moon.

The caribou had come pawing through the snow banks to feed on the moss-covered land. The walrus had come from the sea to sleep on the rocks along the beach and the men had killed them with clubs of driftwood. The vicious shaggy musk ox had come, too. Its meat was the best tasting of all, but when it bent its head and rubbed its eyes on the inside of its forelegs, the musk ox made a terrible smell. Of all the animals, it was the hardest to hunt. When the hunters appeared, the musk ox did not run away as the caribou did, but stood close together and looked at the hunters. Only those men who threw their spears accurately could kill one of the animals before it made its deadly charge. There had been birds, too, that had come to lay their eggs on the ground and raise their young. And the foxes came to eat them. Even the little porcupine came to eat the fat buds on the dwarf willows. This was the land Throw Stone knew. This was home. But now the animals were gone.

The boy and the Father were dressed in their warmest and best clothing. Over skin trousers, they wore fur trousers with the fur turned out. The trousers fitted over heavy skin boots that were tied around their ankles with leather thongs. Their loose one-piece fur tops reached below their knees. Hoods were attached to the fur tops, but now they walked bare-headed and without mittens so they would not perspire. Their mittens of soft animal skin were tied together and hung from a loop over their shoulders.

They walked slowly in full pack and as they trudged forward, the familiar country behind them faded. But the landscape remained frozen and dreary and the rose-colored sun still hung close to the ground no matter how far they walked.

Finally, when the boy was gasping for breath from weariness,

25

the Father stopped near a snow bank. It was deeper than any the boy had ever seen in the summertime. Here, where the crusted surface curved over them like a domed snowhouse, they sat cross-legged on the cold ground. Throw Stone tugged at his big fur pants which kept falling away from his slim hips. The pants had belonged to his grandfather and hadn't been used for a long time. Since no woman was along to sew new ones when Throw Stone grew taller, his father had made him wear the big ones.

"You will grow into them," his father had said. "When you are a hunter."

This made Throw Stone know all the more that they'd be gone for a long time. Beside him lay his grandfather's hunting spear with its heavy bone point in the end. It was longer than the one his father had made for him, and he was proud to be equipped with the hunting gear of a man.

They ate. Throw Stone broke off a piece of dried meat that was hard as a twig of driftwood. He chewed it until it softened and washed it down with water from the snow-filled bag he carried next to his stomach. The dried meat made him feel stronger, but he wished he had the red meat they ate at home.

"Father," he said. "How long will we walk?"

The Father's brows drew together. "We must walk until we can walk no more. Then we will sleep. Each walk must be at least as far as you can see a hunter on the frozen ice." Throw Stone sighed. These were the Long Walks. (They would be over ten miles long as we measure today.)

"How many walks will we make before we reach the Land Where the Sun Lives?" he asked.

The Father shook his head sadly. "I do not know. I have never been to the Land Where the Sun Lives. How can I know how far it is?"

"Father, are you afraid?"

For the first time in the boy's life, he saw his father tremble. And he didn't answer the question.

To himself, Throw Stone said, "We're both afraid, but we won't talk of it. I have my grandfather's charm stone to protect us."

The wind howled outside the snow bank. Throw Stone felt sad. He thought of his mother and the warm room with the flame in the clamshell and his dog with its nose in its paws. He was cold and stiff, homesick and afraid, but he must hide all these things from his father.

The Father said, "We do not have a house. We do not have a fire. Take off your coat and turn it inside out so the fur will be next to your body."

Throw Stone obeyed, watching the Father remove his coat, too.

"Why don't we build a fire, Father?"

"Because we must hunt," said the Father. "The fire would scare away the animals. This snow bank will be our fire. It can save our lives. If we sleep close together, our bodies will keep us warm."

"Even if we had no furs?" asked the boy.

"No. If we lay naked under the snow we would freeze."

The Father and boy huddled together. Just as the Father said, it was almost as warm as a house and a fire!

Throw Stone dreamed of Yodi. He dreamed he heard him howling as he bounded over the ground. The boy sat bolt upright and listened, awake now. Could it have been Yodi and not a dream? His father stirred.

"Did you hear it, Father?"

"Hear what?"

"It sounded like the howl of a dog."

The Father said, "You are dreaming."

Throw Stone lay down again and listened to the howl of the cold wind, the howl that rolled far, far into the emptiness.

"I dreamed it," he told himself.

But when they awoke to eat the meat again, Throw Stone could hardly swallow for thinking of the dream. What if Yodi had chewed the skin rope in two? Dog That Bites had done it once. What if Yodi was following them? What would he eat on the long journey? He would either starve or go wild if the boy didn't feed him.

While the Father was loading his pack, the boy took a piece of meat from his bag and hid it behind a rock. If Yodi was following, he would find it. Throw Stone was thankful there hadn't been deep snow or the dog would be lost—if he were trying to follow.

They walked again along the rocky way until Throw Stone longed to say he could walk no more.

"How big is the land, Father? It goes on and on and there's nothing beyond but more of the same. I'm ready to turn back."

He looked at his father's stern face. The scar across it was fiery red. The question was not answered.

They continued to walk. Later they ate and slept again under a deep snow bank that stood free of the sloping ground beneath. Here it was warm, but away from it the wind howled. Tired as he was, Throw Stone dragged himself away from the warmth and searched for Yodi's tracks. He saw nothing. Then he went back to the snow bank where his father was huddled asleep. In this vast country, his father looked no bigger than a small animal hiding in the snow.

When they moved on, the boy again hid meat for the dog. They saw neither animals nor tracks of animals. There was nothing but the wind howling and the sound of their own heavy breathing in the cold air. Sometimes at the resting places Throw Stone slept. Then he felt ready to walk again. Sometimes he lay huddled and cold against his father staring at the red sun and wondering if he would live long enough to reach the Land Where the Sun Lives that his grandfather had heard about. He didn't dream of Yodi again, but at each resting place he left a piece of meat.

Throw Stone didn't remember how many times they had slept since they had left home, but he knew they had walked far. The land changed. No longer was it like the rocky hills and coarse

28

sandy beach near the sea. Now it was flattened and crossed with small ice-covered streams that came from rocky bluffs backed by steep hills. Sometimes when the clouds went away, the mountains could be seen far to the west. Their dark grey slopes came out of the grey sky and were lost in the snow-covered hills. Dwarf willow grew knee-high along the stream banks, but it was brittle and without buds, and there was no sign of animals feeding on it.

They had traveled far beyond the homeland—fifteen Long Walks—and had been walking for most of the last moon of summer. Yet, even here, there was no summer. The wind began to grow colder and the sun was no longer always in the sky.

They crawled under a rocky bluff and when Throw Stone caught his breath, he said: "Father, I'm hungry."

"Then eat some of the meat you have carried."

"There isn't any more," he said. His father looked at him sternly as he explained: "I left it all for Yodi, in case he followed."

"For Yodi—a dog? You did this? Look in my bag. It is empty. We have eaten all that I carried. And you have thrown yours away!"

His father huddled into a tight ball. "We will rest and then we must hunt."

Throw Stone's heart was pounding hard in his chest. He had left meat for Yodi when maybe the dog wasn't following at all! And now they would go hungry.

"Father, I have seen no animals, no birds, no tracks of anything . . ."

But his father didn't answer. He was asleep.

THE HUNT

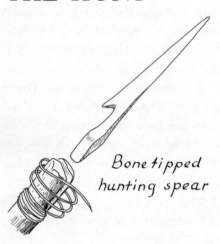

Bone tipped hunting spear

A HEAVY SNOW had fallen while they slept. The Father woke up and shook his head. "This should be the warm time. There should be plants and leaves. Acaba has surely ruined the land. It is turned to ice and snow forever."

As Throw Stone crawled from where he had slept, his father told him, "Put on your goggles, cover your head with your hood. Draw on your mittens. When I have checked my bone points, we will hunt."

Throw Stone drew on his mittens. They were the new ones his mother had made for him a short time before the journey. His fingers fit together in the rounded end of the mittens and there was a thumb place on both sides of each mitten.

"Father," he said curiously. "Why does my mitten have two thumb places? I have only one thumb on each hand."

"Yes, and while you are trying to figure out which way to pull on your mittens, your hands can freeze."

"Oh," said the boy, taking up his spear. He felt it for balance the way his grandfather used to do.

For the hunt, Throw Stone and his father each arranged two of the bone points in their belts. The tips of the points were slanted down to the left so that they might be drawn out quickly to replace those on their spears. The carrying bags were left at the sleeping place.

Grasping their spears with mitten-covered hands, the boy and his father moved away from the rocky bluff. The Father was ahead. They walked carefully, stopping often to look in all directions. The sky was grey and there were gusts of fine snow.

They reached the crest of a broad ridge beyond which was an ice-covered stream larger than any they had yet crossed. To the left the rocky bluff was hidden in haze. To the right was a flat snow-covered country. They moved forward, following alongside the winding ice-covered stream.

There was no sound but the crunch of their snowshoes breaking through frozen snow. Throw Stone's stomach ached from hunger. He said nothing to his father, but tightened his belt.

They continued to walk, to stop and to search until Throw Stone's mittened hands hurt from clutching the spear.

"We'll find no game," he kept thinking. "We'll die of hunger here in the strange country." How he longed to be at home!

They made a wide circle and turned back toward the rocky bluff. Suddenly the Father threw himself flat in the snow and motioned to the boy. Throw Stone fell flat behind him, not knowing what the Father had seen. The Father looked carefully in every direction, then rose slowly to his feet. Throw Stone followed. Now he knew what it was!

31

To their right, were their own snowshoe tracks. They had made a complete circle and were back to the rocky bluff. But, intermingled with their tracks were others—the prints of a bear! Except for being much larger, the hind paw prints were like the footprints of a barefoot man. The bear's big padded front feet had left prints that sank deeply into the soft snow.

They were being followed by a large bear! Throw Stone searched the horizon but saw nothing.

"A bear that can hide in the snow must be the white bear that hunts on ice," Throw Stone told himself. "If only there was something dark, I could see him against the darkness. But the sun is so dim, we can't see him even when he moves!" Throw Stone trembled. He was on his first bear hunt.

Throw Stone and the Father were to start in earnest a game that the boy had often played in the bright moonlight of the dark winters long ago. He had played it with two companions when the snow was freshly fallen on the broad beach by the sea. This was before the boys had gone away with their families. One boy would cover himself with the skin of a white fox and play the part of the white bear. He would try to creep up on the others without their seeing him. At the same time, the other two tried to get within touching distance of the "bear" with their short hunting spears of crooked driftwood. The boys had always imagined the hunt was a real one, and somebody always got killed —the hunters or the bear.

Now he and his father were joined in a real game of death with a bear. They followed the evenly-paced bear tracks in the snow that told them the bear was trailing by scent. The Father and boy again tightened their belts that held the bone points. They separated. Leaving the old tracks that led away from the bluff, they turned back toward it. The Father stopped, looked all around, and stamped on the snow with his snowshoes. This

32

was the signal for Throw Stone to begin circling him. Neither had spoken since the bear's tracks had been discovered.

"Bear hunts are silent and lonely," Throw Stone told himself.

Slowly he circled the Father who kept turning on the hard packed snow to face him. The boy watched his father, at the same time watching in every direction for the invisible bear.

When he had completed the circle and returned to his own tracks, he stopped and turned, stamping on the snow to make it firm. Now, he stood in one place and let his father, who was watching intently, circle him. When the Father returned to his starting place, Throw Stone knew it was his turn to circle again. He began to tremble and his mouth felt dry. How long could he go on this way? How many circles could he make knowing that a hungry bear was following either him or his father?

He began to circle again and had almost completed the circle when he stopped abruptly. The bear's tracks had crossed his path! Throw Stone turned quickly and retraced his steps to signal that he'd seen the bear tracks. The boy took only three steps when he again stopped, signaling that the bear walked on only three paws as it stalked—with the other paw it covered the tip of its black nose and eyes so that it couldn't be seen!

Neither Throw Stone nor his father had seen the bear. Had one of them seen it, he would have knelt to signal the other. The bear lay hidden in the snow. The boy continued to retrace his tracks until he reached his starting place. Then he went on until he came to the place where he'd turned back.

He did not cross any other tracks made by the bear. His heart began to pound and his throat was so dry he couldn't swallow. The bear lay hidden somewhere in the circle he'd made around his father and there was only a short distance between the two of them. Throw Stone stood still and tried to see the bear move in the grey light. He saw nothing.

Then the Father shifted his spear to his left hand, lowered it and pointed it at the boy. A shiver went through him. His father saw the bear. He, Throw Stone, was being stalked!

The boy knelt and pushed the blunt end of his spear into the snow until it struck the hard ground. The sharp end pointed toward the Father. He braced the shaft tightly with his hands. He knew the bear would suddenly burst from the snow where it lay hidden. Now he could only wait until the bear was ready to make its rush. If he could hold his spear steady, the bear would drive itself onto the point. It had to work this way! If it did, while the bear fought at its wound, the boy would have time to get away and the Father would rush in with his spear and kill the animal.

"I have to let the white bear kill itself on my spear," he told himself. But he wondered if he would be brave enough to hold his spear while the bear charged—and not drop it in fright and run.

"Grandfather," he whispered. "Help me now."

He waited. Nothing happened. He strained his eyes in the direction of his father, trying to see the bear between them. His arms ached from clutching the spear. Maybe the bear had decided to let him tire, he thought, and was stalking him in the same way it hunted the seal—waiting for it to go to sleep and then springing.

Then he saw the Father move a step closer and he knew that while he could not see the white bear that lay hidden in the snow with its black nose and eyes covered with its paw, the Father was watching the animal's brown rump, dirty from sitting on the ground.

And, Throw Stone knew that each time the Father moved a step closer to him, the bear had moved a step closer. Now the Father was so close the boy could see the spear's bone point that pointed toward him.

34

Throw Stone whispered: "Father," and tried to swallow again, but he couldn't. His hands were rigid around the shaft of the spear.

The Father shouted, and the snow burst up so near Throw Stone's face that instead of seeing the bear, he only felt the heavy jolt as it struck against the spear. He staggered and rose to his feet. The bear roared. Then he saw it—a great white monster with mouth agape, blood pouring from where the point stuck high in its chest. The bone point was in the bear! It had pulled free as it was supposed to do.

The bear half turned toward the Father, who then drove in the point of his spear, close behind the bear's left shoulder. He pulled his spear shaft free. Quickly Throw Stone drew an extra point from his belt and placed it on the end of his spear. The Father circled the bear and moved toward the boy, as he replaced the point of his spear. The bear was still between them, sunk almost to its belly in the deep snow.

At the end of its long neck, the bear's small head swayed from side to side looking at first the Father, then the boy, as blood spurted from its two wounds.

"It doesn't know which one of us to charge!" thought Throw Stone.

The bear lurched toward the boy; Throw Stone knelt again and thrust his spear shaft in the ground. But before the bear reached him, the Father had again thrust his spear, and another long bone point was buried deep in the bear's side. The animal fought at its wounds with both front paws. Then, as the Father and boy watched, the bear slumped to a sitting position, and crumpled to its side. The bear was dead, once more hidden in the soft snow except where the bloodstained fur was red.

The Father prodded the limp body with the end of his spear.

"It is finished," he said.

37

The two thrust their spears into the deep snow, points to the sky.

The Father clasped the boy's arm. "You hunted well, my son. I am proud of you."

The boy smiled. "Thank you, Father." Then he touched his hunting pouch which held the charm stone. "And thank you, Grandfather."

Polar bear tracks
crossing snow shoe tracks

ALONE

*Flaked cutting or
skinning knife*

"THIS BEAR is old," said the Father. "The meat will be tough.
But it will keep us alive."

"Yes," said Throw Stone. "But eating tough meat like this
will wear down our teeth so we'll have only stubs in our mouths
like my grandmother."

Removing their mittens, they worked loose the three bone
points from the bear's body, then skinned the animal with their
knives and licked the blood from their fingers. They ate some of
the warm heart, for it gave them the courage and strength of
the animal they'd killed. They stacked the other eatable internal
parts of the bear on the skin and dragged it back to the bluff,

leaving the rest of the carcass in the snow where the animal had been skinned.

At the shelter, the Father said: "Bury the poisonous liver beneath a rock. If other animals come, we do not want them to die from eating this liver."

Throw Stone quickly buried the liver, thinking especially that if Yodi *should* be following, he mustn't find it.

"Father, why is the white bear liver bad when the livers of other animals are good?"

"I do not know everything," said the Father. "There must be evil magic in the white bear's liver."

They unloaded the internal parts and stacked them against the bluff. Then they spread the bear skin on the ground with the fur up. The Father crawled inside his fur clothing, lay on the bear skin and covered himself with it. He went to sleep. Too drowsy to stay awake, the boy, too, crawled into his furs and huddled close to his father in the warmth of the bear skin.

Again Throw Stone dreamed that he heard Yodi—or was it some other animal attracted by the smell of the bear meat? He awoke. He looked all around him and toward the place where the carcass of the bear had been left in the snow. He saw nothing but felt joyful. Maybe Yodi was somewhere near, jumping his way through the deep snow, following the smell of the fresh bear meat. Throw Stone lay awake a long time hoping to hear his dog.

When he awoke again, he was alone. The thick fur was cold in the place where his father had slept. What had gone wrong that his father left without speaking to him? Was he hunting? And if so, why—when they had just killed the bear and there was plenty of meat? The boy arose, slung his hunting pouch from his shoulder, put on his goggles and took his spear in his mitten-covered hand. The low sun made a shimmering glare on the snow as far as he could see, but the skin goggles, with only a slit for light, cut out most of the glare. He shivered and clutched his spear. It was the first time he'd been alone in the vast wilderness. The silence was so terrible he stamped in the frozen snow just to hear a noise. He'd heard his grandfather tell how hunters, lost and alone, had gone crazy from the silence. They would run screaming through the wilderness dropping all their gear until they fell into a crevice and were killed or ran onto weak ice, broke through and were drowned.

He shouted into the empty wasteland before him. "Father!" There was no answer. He ran to the base of the rocky bluff, stepped into his snowshoes and walked downward into the thick snow. He reached into his hunting pouch and touched the charm stone.

"Help me," he whispered.

He found the carcass of the bear covered with fine crystals of ice. It was white as the snow.

"I must work," he said aloud. He longed to look for his father's tracks and follow them, but he knew this would displease him. He removed his snowshoes, took out his knife and began hacking the cold hard meat into pieces small enough to carry. The meat was heavy and slippery with fat. He tied it with skin thongs he took from his hunting pouch, and dragged it toward the rocky bluff. He could only pull it a short distance before stopping and removing the snow that piled against it.

When he finally reached the rocky bluff, his father hadn't returned. What if he'd gone away like the Grandfather? What would Throw Stone do?

He made many hauls until all the meat was at the shelter. The work kept him from thinking about being alone. He looked for his father's tracks and found that they led beyond the frozen stream. But he dared not follow. He gathered some rocks and threw them along the icy surface to hear the sound. He'd done this long ago in the homeland where the sea ice was smooth.

That was how he'd gotten his name. He put some of the rocks in his hunting pouch and returned to the bluff.

"I'm alone," he said aloud. Then he ate some of the red meat. He was tired and sleepy but afraid to sleep. What if he were in the land of the evil Acaba who was red and woolly and—how big? As big as the rocky bluff?

"I must do something. I'll build a shelter to protect myself and the meat."

He found the biggest rocks he could lift and made a wall to close in the space around the bear skin. He built another enclosure for the meat. Sleepy and afraid, he crawled behind the stone wall. More than anything, he wanted a fire. But the only wood he'd seen was the low dwarf willows that grew at the edge of the ice-covered stream. He'd seen no moss. Even if he found moss and could manage to set it afire, it would make a big smoke.

"*Can* I make a fire," he wondered. "I don't really know." At home the oil flame had always burned during the long dark winter and in the summer there was the driftwood fire outside.

"I wonder if I could burn a wick in the bear's fat as my mother burned a wick of twisted moss in seal's fat?" But he had neither moss for a wick nor a shell for a lamp. Besides, that was women's work. He had become a hunter and hunters didn't use a fire when they were hunting. Was his father hunting? He didn't know.

He huddled in his furs and tried not to go to sleep. Suddenly, he heard a low moaning sound. It could have been the wind, but then it came again, closer.

Throw Stone reached for his spear. He stood up and shifted the spear in his hand. His heart pounding hard, he moved away from the wall. The moaning began again, but—no—it wasn't a moan—it was a howl! His fear changed to excitement.

"Yodi!" he called.

The excited dog came leaping through the deep snow. Throw

42

Stone hugged him. Then his hand touched the piece of twisted dry skin around the dog's neck.

"You chewed your leash in half! You bad dog!" said Throw Stone. "But I'm glad you're here." He hugged the dog again and fed him.

"My father will be angry with you for following. I hope he won't make you go back." Holding the dog in his arms, Throw Stone climbed into the warm furs. The sun was bright. He moved close to the shadow of the wall so he wouldn't get sun-burned while he slept. Then he fell asleep.

When he awoke, his father was still gone. He and Yodi ate and afterwards they ran and played together in the glaring white snow. The sun shone brightly. The dog wallowed in the deep snow, and shook the dry flakes from his long fur. The boy stripped off his fur clothes and cleaned his naked body by rubbing it with handfuls of the powdery flakes. Then he groped his way back from the glaring snow to the shelter. Again dressed in his furs, he and Yodi ate and slept.

When Throw Stone awoke from his second sleep, the Father was still missing. Even with Yodi close by his side and his grandfather's charm stone in his hunting pouch, he was afraid.

"We must find my father," he told Yodi. "Something has happened to him." The dog answered by wagging his bushy tail.

They trailed the Father's tracks beyond the ice-covered stream. There the snow drifted over them and they faded away.

"The tracks are gone," said Throw Stone. "Go, Yodi, find my father."

The dog ploughed through the snow ahead of him, leaping and howling. They hadn't gone far when Yodi stopped at a rounded snow bank. He whined and dug in the deep snow. Throw Stone helped him dig. In the snow bank he saw his father huddled in his furs.

"Father!" called the boy.

45

The Father stirred and turned his face toward Throw Stone staring with blank eyes.

"I cannot see," said the Father. "I had gone to scout the land beyond the stream while you slept, but I lost my goggles and the snow has blinded me. I could not see to find my way back. How did you find me?"

"Yodi found you."

"Your dog? Your Yodi is here?"

"Yes, Father. He chewed his leash and followed us."

"Then I *did* hear his howl," the Father said. "He has saved my life."

"You won't try to send him back to the homeland alone?"

"No," said the Father. "He would never make it. Besides, he can help carry the meat."

Throw Stone led his father across the frozen stream back to the shelter. The Father rested under the bear skin while Throw Stone fed him chunks of the meat.

The Father said, "We will have to stay here until I can see again."

"Yodi and I will hunt."

"No," the Father said. "There are no signs of animals—I went far to find them. There are none."

"But the white bear—"

"It was hunting far from the sea just as we have come far from the homeland. It was an old male that had strayed away to live alone. After I have rested, we must go on."

"Yes, Father," said Throw Stone. Now that Yodi was with him, he longed to reach the land where the animals lived.

"I know my grandfather's spirit follows me in the charm," he told Yodi. "But am I the one who will have to fight Acaba?"

THE SNOWHOUSE

*Flint struck against
meteoric iron produces sparks*

EVEN THOUGH the Father was snow-blind, he still told Throw
Stone what to do.

"Make the fire," said the Father.

"Me?" replied Throw Stone, surprised. "I've never made one
before—not alone."

"Make it," said the Father.

Throw Stone gathered brushy willow twigs and dead roots and
stacked them high. He crumpled some of the smallest dry
branches and piled them like a bird's nest. Over a piece of dry
moss that lay close to the crumpled branches, he struck his two
fire rocks together again and again. Finally a spark caught the

moss. Blowing on it gently, he coaxed it to life. All at once the moss crackled with a flame that jumped to the dry branches. He'd done it!

"You see?" he whispered as if Strong Girl were there to hear. "I *can* make a fire."

He kept the fire burning against the rocky bluff; the stone wall reflected the heat. Here they slept and ate many times.

While the Father rested against the stone wall, Throw Stone stripped the bear skin of the fatty meat. It would be light to carry and would sustain them on the long walk ahead.

Using the skin of the bear's legs he made a carrying pack for Yodi to haul a load of meat.

They ate much of the meat. Some of it Throw Stone cut into thin strips and hung high on the face of the bluff to dry in the smoke from the fire.

"We'll carry this meat with us," he told Yodi. "And you have a new carrying pack to haul your part." What was left would remain frozen at the shelter as a "cache" covered with stones and marked by crossed sticks, so the family would have a place to get meat on the return trip. The stones would protect the meat from the animals; the crossed sticks, tied together and stuck in the ground, showed ownership if other of The People came that way.

How Throw Stone wished some of The People *would* come along! Were he and the Father the first of The People ever to come to this land? The Grandfather had told of a strange hunter that came to the homeland long ago. But had he traveled as far as this?

Throw Stone took the sinews from the forelegs of the bear. He and the Father put them inside their clothes. Next to their warm bodies the sinews would soften and could be used as new wrappings for the spears. Then, using pieces of bear skin, the boy made snow goggles for his Father and snow boots for Yodi.

He sharpened the long bone points they used to kill the white bear. By scraping them with thin chips of stone struck from the skinning knives, the tips became like the needles the women used to sew clothing. He put the sharpened points into the spears and the old sinew was rewound with some of the new. To repair their snowshoes he used strips of skin he had rubbed with fatty meat. Afterwards, they ate the meat.

"I'm working like a woman," Throw Stone told the Father. "When you can see again, you'll call me Strong Girl."

The Father shook his head and rubbed his snow-blind eyes. "I wonder if Dark Hunter and his family are still alive?" he said. "It would be comforting to know that far west in the mountains Dark Hunter lives and will one day come to meet us."

"Do you really think we'll see him again, Father?"

"No," the Father answered.

It was now the end of summer. They had been away from the homeland a full moon. Each day, the sun hung lower in the sky; and each time it went out of sight, it stayed away longer. The ground was blown nearly bare of the snow. One day the Father said, "Now I can see. We must go on."

First they trimmed the bear hide for a sleeping skin, just large enough to cover them as they lay on part of it. This was rolled tightly and strapped on Yodi's back, and the trimmings from the skin were added to the cache of meat. On Yodi's back was also added the carrying pack made from the skin of the bear's legs, partly filled with some of the dried meat. Yodi sat nearly hidden by his big load and Throw Stone wondered if he could carry it.

The Father and boy then filled their bags with the rest of the dried meat and carried the bags by straps hung across their foreheads. They moved away from the rocky bluff that had been their home for many sleeps, followed by Yodi, who struggled along with his legs spread wide apart.

49

"We travel like the women," Throw Stone said, "bent forward under our heavy loads. All we can see is the ground."

They trudged forward. The land was tufted with small hard plants that made them lose footing. The plants grew so close together the Father and boy couldn't help stepping on them. Their feet slipped forward, sideways and backwards. Throw Stone's legs ached, but he said nothing. Finally the Father stopped, squatted down and touched the inside of his legs.

"My legs are swollen and hard. This must be more of the bad magic of Acaba."

"Shall we stop and build a fire so you can rest?"

"No," said the Father. "We must reach the new land quickly." He rose and stretched his legs. He moved on, again slipping and sliding as he walked.

After many walks, the loads of meat grew lighter. Still they hadn't seen animals. The first winter moon was now in the sky and they sometimes walked by moonlight and starlight. They slept where they found clumps of willow, for here they were able to build fires which smoldered deep into the dead roots. After each sleep, they awoke to find the sun hanging a little lower in the sky, and soon it was only a glow to one side of the horizon. Wind blew the snow in a cloud around their feet and up into their faces. The snow was as hard and sharp as the sand on the beach near the homeland sea. It seemed always to come from the ground or from some place not far off, never from the sky.

Soon there were many willow thickets along the banks of the frozen streams and the ground was covered with deep-crusted snow. Often they traveled on the slippery surface of the streams walking with snowshoes spread wide apart to keep their footing. The sky was snow filled. They were heading for the Land Where the Sun Lives and yet Throw Stone had never been so cold! Under his bundle of fur and meat Yodi trudged behind in their

50

tracks. Only the sight of the dog kept up the boy's courage.

The sky grew strange. A dark wall of grey rose between the snow and the sky. In every direction Throw Stone looked, the wall was still there. It moved ahead of them and followed behind, always remaining the same distance.

Now there were white bark trees as white as the snow—and so many of them! Throw Stone had never imagined trees could grow so tall! Nothing in the homeland reached so high in the sky. If only he weren't tired, how much he could enjoy all these new things. But with each step he took, he felt as if he were lifting more than his whole body on each snowshoe. He stumbled and fell.

Finally the Father said, "We will build a snowhouse and rest."

They climbed to a high snowy ridge where the tall straight trees were less crowded and the wind seemed to come from far away. Here they found a smooth surface of hard snow and marked off a circle. With the Father's long bladed knife, they cut blocks from the inside of the circle. The blocks were a little thicker than the Father's longest finger, as long as the Father's arm, and as wide as half the arm. They made a circle of the blocks by placing them on edge, each slightly sloping toward the center. Then, using the first row as a base, they placed the other blocks upon it, building them round and round in a spiral until they formed a dome. The last block in the dome was cut to leave a hole for smoke to escape. All the cracks were chinked with loose snow so that the walls would become one solid piece of ice. For the entrance, the Father and boy cut a low tunnel below floor level.

All the gear was put inside. The meat Yodi had carried was hung high in a tree to protect it from the wolves and bears—and from Yodi. The dog lay in the snow nearby, his legs curled under him. Throw Stone and his father dragged a large flat rock up the slope and into the snowhouse. They placed it in the mid-

51

dle of the room and the Father made a fire on top of it. After they ate, they spread the bear skin on the floor and slept on it.

"We must hunt," said the Father when they awoke.

They walked far across the high ridge searching in all directions, but saw neither animals nor tracks of animals. They walked through a valley and onto another ridge but the snow was smooth and unmarked except for their own snowshoe tracks in which Yodi followed. Returning to the snowhouse after each hunt they ate and slept. The meat dwindled to the load that had been carried by the dog.

They had been gone from the home by the sea for more than a moon. (And they had walked more than 300 miles.) Throw Stone wondered how much farther they must go. Their hair had grown over their eyebrows and they hacked it away with their skinning knives.

The Father's mouth was grim. "This is not the place where we make our home. We must move on."

"Yes, Father," said Throw Stone. He was beginning to wonder if they would ever find animals again. They were far, far from the homeland and they had found nothing but one stray bear. What if the Grandfather had been wrong? What if there were no animals in the land except that one stray bear?

They left half of the remaining bear meat at the snowhouse as a cache, the rest they put into their carrying bags. They moved on, followed by the dog with only the roll of bear skin on his back. At each ridge they stopped and looked for animals. They saw nothing except the white bark trees. The ground was covered with crusted snow which held firm under their snowshoes.

"Father," said Throw Stone. "Can't we turn back? Toward the homeland at least we found the white bear. Here Acaba has frightened away all the animals. I haven't even seen a bird." He tried to smile. "I liked hunting the white bear. Please, can't we go back?"

52

The Father put his hand over the scar on his face and said wearily: "I told you the white bear was an old stray. Say no more of turning back."

They walked long in the dim light before they rested. They made a place for the bear skin on top of small branches broken from the tall trees. With dry limbs from the dead trees, they built two fires and slept between them. Yodi curled himself in a tight ball close to the boy and each was kept warmer by the other. Many times they rested and slept and each time they had less to eat than before. They tightened their belts and drank more of the melted snow from the skin bags they carried next to their bare bodies. This made their hunger seem less. They rested often and Throw Stone wondered how much longer he could follow his father's tracks.

No longer able to keep close behind his father, he stopped. The dog sat and looked intently into his face.

"I'm afraid, Yodi," said Throw Stone. "The People have eaten dogs when they were very hungry. I hope my father doesn't think of it."

Yodi's only answer was to bare his teeth in a grin. Throw Stone grinned back. "Well, anyway we won't help him think of it."

Skin snow goggles

53

THE MISTS

Yodi's tracks

Wolf tracks

THEY WALKED along the banks of a frozen stream. Strange green trees now grew among the white bark ones. Some had long drooping branches as green as the wing feathers of birds that once came to the homeland; others had twig-like branches covered with small brittle leaves and looked like sticky bushes hung with cones; others had branches that grew wide at the bottom of the trunk, but gradually and evenly narrowed upward on the tree until they ended in a point.

Throw Stone stared at them. "I know almost nothing about trees," he said. "I know brush and driftwood and scrub willow but not trees. Does any animal live in the trees, Father?"

"I do not know," said the Father. "The old people tell stories of birds flying into the trees and the wolverine leaping from the trees."

"I believe I could climb a tree," said Throw Stone, "when I don't have my pack, I'll try. Yodi, can you climb a tree?"

Yodi wagged his tail. Throw Stone laughed. "No, you can't climb a tree. If you could, back at the homeland you'd have climbed the sticks of driftwood where we hung the meat."

They followed along the ridge and came to large boulders like those at the rocky bluff where the white bear had been killed. The haze which had disappeared for a brief interval returned and they could barely see the white bark trees. They brushed past the tall green trees with their branches bent down by a covering of snow and ice. Wind howled in the tree tops.

Once, when the ground haze cleared and the sun shone on the glaring snow, the two saw far ahead. The mountains which had always been to the west now seemed to have moved in front of them. Throw Stone wondered if they were headed in the wrong direction but the Father said nothing. To the east was the dark forest which stretched as far as they could see.

Timidly, Throw Stone spoke, "My grandfather said Dark Hunter was to go south by way of the mountains while we went by way of the valley. But we are headed into the mountains! Why is this?"

The Father said, "The mountains must spread to here. Your grandfather told of a way through the valley so it must be true. We will follow the valley and go beyond the mountains."

"Father, will there be bears in the mountains?" The Father didn't answer.

"We're both so hungry now," thought Throw Stone. "We can't think of bears—except perhaps to think of bear meat."

Grey mists clung to the ground and they walked among the enormous boulders and rocks covered by snow except for bare patches of grey where the wind had blown the snow away. Green trees grew among the rocks. The Father could no longer lead in a straight path. He weaved to right, then left, working his way among the trees, rocks and boulders. Everywhere the ground was covered with crusted snow. They were many, many walks from the homeland. (400 miles as we would measure.)

Yodi whined and crouched down. The Father moved cautiously to a cluster of boulders, his spear held high. Throw Stone saw nothing. The Father rushed in among the boulders, then drew back in horror. Throw Stone hurried after him to look for himself but the Father caught his arm, held him and covered the boy's eyes with his mittened hand.

"No," said the Father. "Do not look." He led Throw Stone away from the cluster of boulders. "A dead wolf—I saw it—its evil spirit will follow us. But you did not see it?"

"No," said Throw Stone.

"No," said the Father. "Its carcass fell through the crusted snow. You did not see . . ."

The Father crouched close to the ground. "Leave me," he said. "Walk a short distance and wait."

Throw Stone did as his father told him. He faced toward the mountains and tried not to turn around, but his curiosity was too much for him. He took a quick look at the Father. He was still crouched, mumbling to himself. Of course! The Father would have a charm stone passed on to him by *his* grandfather. Why hadn't he thought of it before?

When the Father joined the boy, his face was drawn and grey. "Now you know why we never kill the wolves," the Father explained. "It is for fear one of The People may find a dead one— the worst of all evil magic."

They walked again, both so tired and hungry they could scarcely move. Soon they heard a roaring. It grew louder. Throw

56

Stone thought of the homeland and the sound the wind made when it blew the sea water to the shore. But here the grey mists billowed around them. He could barely see the Father, Yodi, the rocks and the trees.

The Father stopped to listen. "It must be the river."

"The big river, Father?" asked the boy, thinking of Acaba.

The Father lowered his head and walked on through the mists, moving toward the sound until they came to a dense growth of willows. Throw Stone felt spray in his face, like the spray from the sea in the homeland. The roaring sound grew louder.

"Take off your snowshoes," said the Father. "We cannot walk with them in this thick brush."

Snowshoes in hand, they struggled through the brush with Yodi at their heels. When the trees thinned they stopped to see what lay before them. Beyond the trees was a sand bar like that they had known along the sea. But the sand was tan-colored like the caribou. The roaring sound grew louder. It came from the direction they were going!

The Father turned back toward the willow trees, and again they were among rocks and boulders. They could scarcely see each other and they stumbled against rocks and trees.

"Father, can't we build a fire and wait until the mist is gone?"

The Father's voice was shrill. "No! Evil magic is upon me. I must leave this place where I found the dead wolf."

Again they wandered in the mist and this time they came to a grey rocky cliff that rose so high its top disappeared in the haze. The Father leaned against the cliff, his arms outstretched. He felt his way along the cliff in one direction, then the other.

"This is the end," he said. "We cannot climb over the mountains. The evil magic of the wolf has finished me."

The Father sat down and buried his face in his hands.

57

Throw Stone stood in the mist looking at his father and wondering what to do. From his hunting pouch, he drew out the charm stone and brought it close to his face.

"Lead us through the valley," he said. Then he thought of the sand bar. Did it end against the mountain or go beyond?

"Father," he said. "I have good magic and I did not see the dead wolf. Follow me."

"I am finished," said the Father without raising his head.

Throw Stone tied a leather thong around Yodi's neck and gave the free end to the Father. "Here. Hold this. Yodi will lead you and he will follow me."

The Father rose and obeyed like a child. The boy listened for the roaring sound and walked in that direction. He worked his way through the willows along the sand bar. He turned. Dimly he saw that Yodi was leading his father. The farther Throw Stone went along the sand bar, the louder was the roar. The mists swirled around them, and again there were boulders. The sand at his feet was wet with the mist and free of snow. The rocky cliff again appeared, rising high above the great boulders at its base. With his right hand Throw Stone could reach out and touch the rocky face of the mountain. To his left he could see no farther than an arm's length. Now the roaring sound came from almost underfoot.

Then he saw it! Racing water lapped at the great boulders. It was the river! He tried to call to the Father but his voice was drowned by the roar of the water. He felt his way along the face of the cliff with the water almost at his feet. Throw Stone held his breath, hoping the Father wouldn't stumble and fall into the fast water and be lost.

He followed along the river's edge until the cliff no longer crowded him toward the water. Again there was the wide sand bar, now free of boulders. He turned and looked. His father was safe, still being led by Yodi.

58

They had left the roar of the running water; they had left the heavy mists that rose from it in the cold air. Beyond, willows grew close together along the sand bar and green trees spread out over the broad valley.

"We've made it," said Throw Stone.

The Father stood beside him. "Yes. We have overcome the evil magic of the dead wolf." The shrillness had gone from his voice.

They built a fire, rested and talked of the evil magic they had escaped. Then again they walked. Soon they came to a thick clump of tall green trees where snow was piled high. Beyond was a single tall tree where lower branches were piled so high with snow that the tree seemed to grow from a large snowhouse. Close by was a small frozen stream.

The Father said, "We must rest here."

They crawled to the trunk of the tall tree below the branches. In the dim light which came through the snow-covered branches, Throw Stone could hardly see the ground. They broke green branches from the tree and spread them on the snow. On this they laid the bear skin.

The Father took out the last small bundle of meat.

"This is all we have to eat," he said angrily. "And the dog must be fed."

Throw Stone hung his head. Already the Father had forgotten that Yodi had saved his life!

THE FOREST HOME

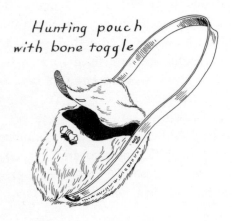

Hunting pouch
with bone toggle

As if Yodi understood the Father's anger, he slunk outside. The boy followed and called to him, but Yodi would not come. He stood before a clump of trees whining strangely. Again Throw Stone called, but Yodi still stood before the trees, head cocked to one side. Then, although Throw Stone could see no animal but the dog, he heard a snort and the stomping of cloven hooves. Still whining, Yodi backed a few steps. He was coaxing an animal to come toward him. Throw Stone sniffed. Musk ox! The musky, long-carrying odor of musk ox!

From between the trees a heavy black musk ox moved slowly into view. He had enormous humped shoulders, side hair that

60

dragged in the snow, a whitish nose and whitish face hair. The animal lowered his massive head with the broad horns which curved sharply downward and then turned up at the tips. The musk ox snorted and stomped again. Yodi howled. And the animal bellowed and charged. At the noise the Father ran out of the shelter. He and the boy grabbed their hunting pouches and spears and raced after the musk ox.

Yodi led the procession onto the frozen surface of the stream. The musk ox clattered after the dog, only to slip and crash on the glossy surface. It made a weak attempt at rising but its hind legs were broken. The man and boy came in for the kill while Yodi bounced happily around the beast he had lured onto the ice.

Now the Father was smiling. "That dog of yours—he is like no other dog I have ever seen. He has the courage of a hunter and now he has delivered this animal to us—a musk ox, the finest of all meats. But," he added, "this musk ox is an old one. Does the old fellow travel alone? Somewhere ahead of us we should find the herd of young."

"Another old animal," said Throw Stone. "My poor teeth. Nothing to eat but tough meat."

They quickly set about skinning the animal, as Throw Stone tried to hold his breath against the musky odor. They ate the heart for this would restore their strength faster than any other meat. Yodi was given all he could eat. When it was completely skinned, the carcass was piled on the skin. The dog's leash was tied to it and the heavy load was moved to the shelter.

They rested at the tree shelter and lit a small fire of dry limbs to brighten the darkness under the green branches. The fire made much smoke and helped dry the strips of red meat that had been cut from the carcass and hung high in the tree branches.

The Father and boy ate the red meat and slept many times. It

61

was now the second moon of winter. They had been away from home for more than two moons.

While they rested, they peeled the fatty flesh from the musk ox skin and dried the fat. They softened the skin by rubbing it with snow and scraping with blunt stones. When they slept on the bear skin they were covered with the musk ox hide. Yodi slept on the skins at their feet and Throw Stone knew his father was glad to have the dog with them, although he never said so.

Once again, it was time to move on. Most of the meat was cached in the tall green tree, and the rest put in the carrying bags. As they traveled, Throw Stone and the Father looked for young musk ox, but found nothing. Yodi followed with his load of two skins.

Two winter moons had come and gone and it was now the third winter moon. (They were more than 45 Long Walks from the homeland.) Even the sun was different in this new land. It didn't hide below the horizon during the winter as it had in the homeland, but was in the sky to greet them, when Throw Stone and his father awoke each day.

"This is very strange for winter!" said Throw Stone. "Grandfather was right. We're going to the Land Where the Sun Lives."

All the familiar things of snow, stars, and moon seemed strange. This was a land of tall green trees that cast patches of shadow on the snow. The shadows made the Father uneasy. He jumped and turned in them, thinking that animals were following him. When at last the northern lights reached high into the sky, the Father and Throw Stone felt less afraid, for this was like the homeland. They loved the shimmering many-colored lights of night which burst from below the horizon and extended high overhead. It was then that the trees and shadows no longer seemed to hide evil things.

Whenever the weather was too bad to travel, the man and boy

rested, or, when the night sky was overcast and the stars could not be seen, they gave up and slept. But, when the sun rose above the horizon and when the night was clear—full of stars and moonlight—they traveled.

They found rabbit tracks that disappeared in the brush. They followed a flock of ravens flying overhead and found shreds of caribou meat and the tracks of a wolf.

"Where are the wolves?" asked Throw Stone. "I have never seen one although I hear their howls in the night and we've found their tracks."

"They are here," said the Father. "But they are hunting as we hunt, so they travel alone."

The third winter moon was almost gone. The travelers walked on.

Throw Stone lagged behind his father and turned to look at Yodi. Even the dog's face seemed sad. "I'm sorry, Yodi," said Throw Stone. "Perhaps we'll travel until we die."

Slowly they climbed a rocky tree-covered ridge. It was quiet among the tall trees. But, far off to the east, Throw Stone heard the screech of the wind and saw the river again. It was frozen now and, at this point, was wider than the boy had ever imagined a river could be. A hazy mist rising from its icy surface blurred the trees on the other side.

"Father," said Throw Stone in amazement, "This is the same river that had the rushing water. Here it is so wide and frozen— could it be the river of Acaba? Is he there on the far side, hiding among the trees?"

The Father said, "We do not know this is the river of Acaba."

Throw Stone nodded but in his heart he knew that it was the river. He thrust his hand inside his hunting pouch to touch the charm stone.

63

"I am tired," said the Father. "We will make a shelter here."

"Please, Father," said the boy. "I'm afraid of the river. Let's walk again."

The Father didn't answer. Instead, he led the way to a tall green tree where they made a shelter, ate, and lay down in the fur skins. Throw Stone no longer heard the sound of the wind from across the river. His father and Yodi lay close at his side, sleeping. The boy, too, fell asleep and there were dreams of the misty river and his grandfather's face as big as the sun rising out of the mist.

When he awoke, his father was making the fire. Throw Stone dressed quickly. The Father emptied the last of the dried meat from his bag and divided it into three parts.

His face was grim. "Take your dog and hunt," he told the boy. "I will stay here and rest."

With spear, hunting pouch, and dog, Throw Stone walked away from the river and into the forest. He passed thick clumps of the white bark trees and saw unfamiliar animal tracks.

Yodi romped ahead. When they reached a wall of willow trees whose slender limbs were burdened to the ground with snow, Throw Stone heard a clucking sound. He stopped to listen, remembering. White birds! It was the sound the white birds used to make in the homeland. Throw Stone searched the area trying to follow the sound. Yodi ran around sniffing until his nose led him into a cluster of small snow mounds. The dog pawed at one and it burst open as a white bird flew up into the air.

Quickly Throw Stone thrust his spear and pulled it back. Fastened to the point was a fluttering ball of white feathers. Then, all around him the snow burst open with flying white birds. They shot straight up from the edge of the trees, only to quickly settle down in the loose snow and begin to burrow again.

Excited, Throw Stone grabbed the rocks from his hunting pouch and hurled first one, then another and another at the moving snow. Yodi rushed at the fluttering birds; many whirred away but Throw Stone had managed to wound four which Yodi killed.

Throw Stone was a hunter on his own!

When he climbed the ridge, he saw even more animal tracks than before. His head was high, as he returned with the four birds.

The Father looked at the birds and nodded. Throw Stone smiled broadly, showing his big teeth and the Father answered his smile with a chuckle. Together they went to look at the nearby animal tracks the boy had seen.

"There are many animals here," said the Father. "Look—the tracks of the musk ox, here a caribou and there—oh yes—always the wolf. See his big tracks? He is after the caribou."

Throw Stone studied the tracks. When the snow was frozen, tracks were easy to recognize, but in loose, powdery snow like this, the tracks were so muddled that all Throw Stone could tell was that *something* had been there.

"Look," said the Father. "The black raven flies overhead. There must be meat nearby. The raven is waiting until after the wolf has made his kill and has eaten his fill. Then he will feast. Yes, here there are many animals. This will be our home."

Throw Stone licked his lips. "Please, Father. Acaba must live across the river. Grandfather warned us. Acaba will try to kill us."

The Father turned away from him. "In this land live the animals that once came to the homeland during the summer moons. We have traveled four moons to find it. We will stay. After I have rested, I and the dog will return for your mother and your grandmother. It will take many moons to go back to the homeland and return again. Your grandmother is old. Your mother and I will have to wait while she rests along the way and we will have to walk slowly with her. The journey will be hard and must

65

be completed while the snow is on the ground. If the summer sun comes and melts the streams, we may never get across them. So I must go soon. You will stay here and wait for our return."

"No—" said Throw Stone softly. It was the first time he'd ever said no to his father, but he was terrified. "No. Don't make me stay here alone. Please take me with you when you go back."

"No," said the Father sternly. "There is not enough meat cached for both of us. Here you can hunt until we return. We are deep into the cold time, but even if I do not return for many, many moons you can live here."

"But you—" said Throw Stone. "You'll be traveling during the darkest winter moons! The land will be nothing but snow. You'll be lost."

The Father put his arm around his son's shoulder. "No. I will find my way by the stars. The People do not get lost. We need no markers. Besides, have you forgotten the good northern lights will help me?"

"But for me—" said Throw Stone. "I'll be alone here with Acaba! Please, please let Yodi stay with me."

"No," said the Father, gently but firmly.

The boy walked down to the frozen river. He tried to see through the haze that rose from the icy surface and hid the forest beyond. Yodi whined at his feet.

"What do you see, Yodi? I'm to be left here all alone with whatever is over there."

And all he'd have left to protect him was the charm stone his grandfather had given him.

FROM ACROSS THE RIVER

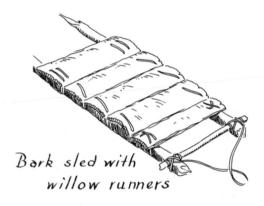

Bark sled with
willow runners

THE FATHER and Throw Stone built a house of tree limbs and covered it with green boughs weighted down with rocks. They enclosed the back of it with an ice wall like they had built for the snowhouse. They covered the ground inside the shelter with green branches and spread out the furs of the bear and musk ox. Before the open end of the shelter they built a fire.

They hunted in their snowshoes; moving rapidly over the hard surface of the crusted snow. Yodi was always ahead of them or alongside the boy; he no longer sank into the snow as he had when it was freshly fallen. His snow boots saved his paws from the sharp frozen snow and he ran as he had on the bare rocky land by the sea. They killed many white rabbits and white birds. Here in the forest the animals were not afraid of hunters.

They returned from the hunts carrying loads of the white rabbits. "We must have more than rabbit meat," the Father said. "We need good red meat of the big animals or we will grow as weak as the rabbits themselves."

They hunted far down their slope to the south and discovered a small frozen stream that ran into the big river. Here the white bark trees were cut down by strange animals that used the limbs and river mud to build small mound houses along the water's edge.

Throw Stone spied one of the animals chewing at a large tree trunk. Bigger than Yodi, the animal had a flat broad tail, a narrow, pointed head and was covered with dark slick hair. He chewed at the tree with bright orange teeth. When he saw the two hunters and the dog, he slapped the ground with his broad tail, making a thump, thump sound, and scurried into the mound house.

Throw Stone leaned down and peered cautiously into the opening of the house; afraid he might get his nose bitten. The animal was gone! It had disappeared into a hole that led under the banks along the edge of the stream.

Later they found the fresh tracks of a caribou where it had fed in a clump of tall willows.

"The caribou is what we want," said the Father.

Father and son separated. Throw Stone knelt in the snow at the edge of the ice-covered stream, his dog beside him.

"Go get the caribou, Yodi," he whispered. "Find him."

The dog sniffed the air and ground and raced into the willows. Throw Stone heard a growl. The willow branches parted and a large caribou ran into the open. It ran to the bank of the frozen stream and paused in fear. Then, hearing Yodi close behind, the caribou fled down the stream, slipping on the icy surface. Throw

68

Stone hurled his spear and drove it deep into the animal's side. The wounded beast stumbled to its knees, rose and hobbled a few steps, then fell dead on the ice.

"You have killed your first big animal all alone," the Father shouted happily to Throw Stone. "Now you are a real hunter!"

They laughed and joked as they skinned the animal. But, while they dragged the meat back to the shelter, the boy kept thinking of Acaba. He imagined the evil one watching from across the river—waiting for the Father to leave.

It was now the fourth moon of the winter, almost five moons since they had left the homeland. (They had traveled over 600 miles.) Their hair hung below their brows, and again they cut it.

They peeled bark from a great white tree and built a sled, binding it with thongs.

"This is Yodi's sled," said the Father. "He must drag the furs and meat back to the homeland."

Again, the boy was reminded that he was to be left alone while his father and Yodi returned for the women. He was homesick to see his mother and grandmother, but he wanted to go, too; not to be left in the land of Acaba!

The sun was low in the sky. When it disappeared, the stars and the moon or, most often, the friendly lights took its place.

The Father and boy killed two more caribou. Some of the meat they cut from the carcasses, the rest they bundled in caribou skins and swung it high in the tall tree beside the shelter. Here it dangled from the end of a braided thong out of reach of the ground animals—and Yodi.

At long last the Father said: "The time has come for me to go. You will help me get the meat back to make a first cache."

"Yes, Father," said the boy.

It was hopeless to try to change his mind. He knew that the meat on the sled and the meat left at the caches along the way must be sufficient for the Father's journey to the sea and his return with the two women. Throw Stone doubted if it would be enough. No wonder his father wouldn't let him go.

"If only Yodi could stay," he sighed.

They started back toward the homeland to make the first cache. The Father walked ahead; Yodi followed pulling the sled loaded with meat and furs. Throw Stone shoved the sled from behind.

They walked until the Father pointed to a shelter at the trunk of a tall tree.

"Here," he said. They rested while the snow piled a fresh blanket on the green branches. Then they buried half the meat beneath a pile of rocks, hoping no animal would dig it out. The sled was again leashed to Yodi.

Throw Stone stood close to his father.

"Father, you're going to the homeland in the dark of the long winter. Because of my grandmother you say you may not be able to return. If you don't, what will I do? Shall I try to find you?"

"No," replied the Father. "If you tried to find me, you would starve. Live at the forest home until you are older. Then search for Dark Hunter and his family. They are somewhere in the mountains."

The boy looked away. "What if Acaba is there in the forest home?"

"Your grandfather's spirit will help you."

The man turned and moved in the direction of the good lights which colored the sky to the north. Yodi pulled the sled and Throw Stone walked a short way shoving the sled from behind.

"Goodbye," said the Father. "Good Luck."

"Good Luck, Father," the boy answered.

Throw Stone turned toward the forest home. He walked a short distance, then looked back at his father and Yodi. The dog was sitting in the snow, whining! He refused to pull the load. The Father shouted at the dog and prodded him with the butt end of his spear shaft but Yodi wouldn't rise. Throw Stone tried not to laugh at the stubborn dog.

The Father shook his head, stooped down and released the dog. He gave him a swat and Yodi bounded joyfully through the snow toward the boy.

The Father called, "He will keep you company while you are alone!" Taking up the leash, the Father pulled the sled himself.

When the Father disappeared in the forest, Throw Stone turned to Yodi, "I must be very careful and watch every step I take or we will get lost in the forest. Who could find us except the red cloud, Acaba?" The dog wagged his tail. "Yes, smart dog. Show me how to get to the forest home."

Their tracks were hidden in the fresh snow, but with the help of Yodi and his grandfather's charm, Throw Stone made his way back to the forest home. He built a fire and he and Yodi ate some of the caribou meat. Later they huddled together on the musk ox skin and slept.

When Throw Stone awoke, the sun was low in the sky. He and the dog walked down to the small stream. He found some tree limbs that had been chewed off by the strange animals.

"We might try to kill one of them," said Throw Stone. "But what if the meat is poisonous like the white bear liver? I wonder: is it animal or fish? It lives on the land and in the water."

Throw Stone dragged the tree limbs back to his camp and built another shelter which he covered with the caribou skins. He stored the meat in the old part of the shelter and covered the open end with fresh green branches. The branches reflected the heat from the fire into the new skin-covered shelter where he slept on the musk ox hide. Yodi slept outside, close to the fire.

Sometimes, when the moon was in the sky or the good colored lights played high above the tops of the trees, the boy and dog hunted for white birds. Once, they hunted along a ridge where there were no trees. Yodi ran ahead, stopped—and as he stood

71

whining—the boy joined him to see what had happened. Close by, he saw snow rabbits hopping playfully down the slope on their big feet.

"Let's catch one," whispered the boy. "Let's not kill it. Let's catch it and see what it's like."

They rushed after the rabbits but the large white animals hopped away as Yodi floundered in the deep snow. Throw Stone plopped down laughing and Yodi returned, panting hard.

"You couldn't catch them," the boy teased. "I'll have to make you some snowshoes like theirs."

The winter moons came and went and still the Father hadn't returned. While he waited at home in the forest, the boy was busy. He peeled the bark from a tall white tree with his stone knife and made a holder to melt snow near the fire for drinking water. He made new snowshoes of straight willow limbs and bound them with thongs. Also from the slender willow limbs he made throwing spears. With a tree trunk as his target, he practiced using the new spears in his sling.

It was now the fifth moon of winter; seven moons since he had seen his mother! After one more moon, it would be spring. The sun climbed higher into the sky and Throw Stone again hacked away the hair that had grown below his brows.

Throw Stone and Yodi spent many peaceful, happy days exploring the forest and the big river. With the coming of spring at hand, Throw Stone's heart was light and happy. Even the thought of Acaba was far from his mind. Then, one day there came from across the river a sound such as the boy had never heard before. It was like a beast snorting, but not like the snorting of the seals in the homeland, nor like the musk ox. It was more like the wind shrieking between rocks. Acaba! The boy stood very still. He felt lost and alone. He reached into his hunting pouch and touched the charm stone.

"Help me, Grandfather."

Trembling, he walked to the edge of the wide frozen river. He looked across but could see nothing except a blur of green forest.

"He is there," said Throw Stone to Yodi. "And we must live by the river until my family returns or they'll never find us."

Willow Ptarmigan

THE TERRIBLE DREAM

Tree cache

SOON Throw Stone knew the forest better than he had known the homeland. Because he was alone, he ventured far. Always Yodi was there to help him find the way home. They hunted rabbits and birds and the boy killed another caribou. He talked to Yodi so he wouldn't go crazy as hunters sometimes did when they were alone. Always he kept the fire burning. With only his fire and dog to keep him company, he remembered the long dark winters in the homeland when he was a child and The People were together. It had been a happy time. The families gathered for dancing and singing and the old people told stories of things that had happened long ago.

76

Sometimes when he crouched in the shelter near his lonely fire, Throw Stone could almost smell the warm bodies of The People as they crowded into a room and hear their laughter and his grandfather's high chanting voice. But when he heard the shrieking of Acaba from across the river, he cringed close to his dog and whispered: "Grandfather, help me." And he would take out his charm stone. These things soothed him so he could eat again; sleep again; hunt again.

Each day, the sun climbed higher in the sky but it was lost behind the hazy mists Acaba sent from across the river. The evil clouds covered all the skies and even the good colored lights of the north were hidden. Snow lay deep on the land. No longer were there many animal tracks as when the Father and the boy had first come to the forest. If it hadn't been for Yodi, Throw Stone could never have found the rabbits which hid in the snow banks.

When the moon was in the sky, white owls flew through the trees and hunted the white rabbits, too. Once a large spotted animal jumped from where it lay hidden in a tree and killed a rabbit playing on the snow. The spotted animal's face was like the great grey owl, with pointed ears and green eyes. When Throw Stone and Yodi followed it as it crept through the snow, it ran away.

Winter passed; the second moon of spring began but the cold wind stayed. Throw Stone had left the homeland almost nine moons before. He had been alone in the forest four moons.

In the darkness he lay bundled in the furs and watched the fire being whipped by the cold screaming wind. For lack of wood the fire flickered and almost went out, but the night was too cold for Throw Stone to crawl out into the wind for more firewood. His nose felt like an icicle already. He hummed to himself as he curled up to sleep. He awoke with a jolt. Was he awake or asleep? He had had a terrible dream. He dreamed he saw the

77

Father, the Mother and the Grandmother lying in the snow, dead and as stiff as tree limbs. Dog That Bites was running around the three bodies whining, trying to wake them up.

Throw Stone opened his eyes wide in terror and looked at the fire. Where were the three bodies? Now he saw only dead tree limbs in the snow. Was it magic? Was his family dead? He called to Yodi who lay huddled at his feet and the dog crawled into the furs with him.

"Are they dead, Yodi?" He put his arms around the dog's neck. "What will become of me? They're dead and I'm alone in this strange country. If only you could speak!" He squeezed the dog's neck hard. "Speak, Yodi!" Yodi whined in answer.

"No, you can't speak. Poor Yodi can't speak. But I have to find someone who speaks. Dark Hunter! My father said if he didn't return to find Dark Hunter. Now I've had a magic dream and they won't return. I'll look for Dark Hunter and his family in the mountains."

He went to sleep again.

When he awoke he made a platform of limbs in a tree and cached all the meat he couldn't carry. Then he crossed two sticks, tied them with sinew and stuck them in the ground to mark his possession of the cache.

"But no one will see it. I wish someone *would* come. Then I wouldn't have to go searching for Dark Hunter in the mountains, just to hear the sound of his voice."

He told Yodi, "We're going to the mountains where the bears live, but we're going *away* from the land of Acaba."

With him he took the sleeping skin, the skin water bag, the hunting pouch, his sling, three spears and as much dried meat as he could lift in the carrying bag. Yodi swayed under the load of skins strapped to his back. They headed for the little frozen stream to the south. When they reached it, they followed it west toward the mountains.

"You'll see," said Throw Stone. "This is a very wise thing to do." But he kept glancing back toward the forest home, wondering if he should still wait for the Father. He hadn't grieved for the Father and the women because he couldn't quite believe the dream. Still, he had to find The People, he had to search for Dark Hunter, and he used the dream as an excuse. How fine it was to be doing something besides waiting!

He walked quickly and the spring sun warmed him. He threw back his hood and drew off his mittens. The air was sparkling fresh and most of the snow had melted from the ground. Even Yodi under his burden of skins seemed excited by the trip. They were headed for the mountains which glistened in the sunshine.

The sun climbed higher. Just ahead, the little stream divided in a wide fork. Throw Stone stopped. Which way to go? Yodi trudged ahead of him down the south fork, and the boy followed. One way was as good as another.

Later, in the darkness Throw Stone crouched next to a windblown fire and told Yodi, "The mountains are farther than I thought. But now we are too far from the forest home to go back."

When morning came, they followed the frozen stream to where the waters spread over the flat ground into a small lake. On the northern shore of the lake grew a few of the white bark trees and the tall green ones, some close to the grassy shore where the snow had already melted. On the southern shore a forest of the green trees grew along a rocky slope. Yodi trotted down the grassy north shore. The mountains looked just as far away. Already they had eaten much of the meat and had walked four Long Walks.

"When we reach the mountains," said Throw Stone, "We may see a bear larger than the white bears. How will we kill it before it gobbles us up?"

They saw a caribou crashing through the trees, but Throw

79

Stone was too loaded with gear to have time to strip down to follow it.

"Dark Hunter will have bear meat to feed us," he told Yodi, then added sadly, "or the bears will have Dark Hunter."

They followed along the grassy shore to the head of the little lake. At a thick clump of junipers, Yodi stopped and whined.

"Rabbits, Yodi?" asked Throw Stone. "Do you smell rabbits? Very well, we'll stop here and get a rabbit." He took off his gear and built a good shelter. Working with his fire rocks he built a roaring fire.

"Let's get a drink of water, Yodi." They went to the grassy shore of the lake. The ice was thin. Throw Stone broke it with a rock and he and Yodi drank.

"I see fish down there," he said. "Big silvery fish. But we're after rabbit."

With his hunting pouch and spear, Throw Stone set out after Yodi. He followed through the forest after the dog until he plopped exhausted on the ground.

"Are you playing with me, Yodi? Are rabbits here?"

He looked up to see a brown bird perched on a bush covered with blue-colored berries. The bird was eating the berries. He thought of killing the bird, then changed his mind. He crawled close to the bush and watched the bird until it flew away. Half afraid, he plucked a berry. If the bird ate it, it must be good food. Caribou ate the moss that grew on the rocks in the homeland and he'd tried eating moss but spat it out for it was filled with dirt. He put the berry in his mouth. It tasted good! It was a taste he didn't know; it was like no meat he had ever eaten, but he liked it! He offered a berry to Yodi but the dog wouldn't touch it.

Throw Stone licked his lips. "Now my grandfather's charm stone is working."

And indeed it was! The boy and dog killed a caribou that came to the grassy shore to drink. They skinned the animal and cut the

legs from the carcass. Throw Stone carried the meat to the shelter in the trees and placed it in the notches of the trees as high as he could reach. They rested. When they walked again, most of the meat was left in the notches of the trees.

Ahead of them Throw Stone saw the grey slopes of the mountains streaked with splashes of green where the trees grew. Snow covered the mountain tops and the sky was blue. The farther they walked, the closer and higher the mountains seemed. Now the stream was nothing more than a series of ice-covered pools filled with large rocks. (The travelers were ten miles from the lake.) The shadow of the mountains covered the area like a dark cloud.

The stone slope opened into a narrow canyon where the stream had once run. Throw Stone looked at the walls of rock around him. "I don't see how we can get through," he sighed.

They struggled up the steep slope of the rocky valley and the canyon walls narrowed. Straight ahead the grey rock cliff shot up high into the sky. Throw Stone leaned back to stare at the top of it. Icicles as big as tree trunks hung from the cliff's edge. He moved a few steps, then turned around searching for an opening. He was blocked off! There was no way to go but back the way they'd come.

Throw Stone sat down and put his head in his arms. What now? He couldn't find Dark Hunter.

"I'm tired," he told Yodi. "And I don't know what to do. I guess we'll go back to the cache by the lake."

Yodi wagged his tail and jumped up against Throw Stone's shoulder. "I hope I can find the way."

He grinned at the dog although he felt sad. "The People never get lost. It is in their blood to find their way in strange country, to find it without markers of any kind." Yodi licked the boy's face.

"I wonder if it is in my blood," he said as he rose wearily to start the journey back to the lake shelter.

MOVING SHADOWS

Wolverine

As HE approached the shelter by the small lake, Throw Stone saw something moving. Yodi looked at him with appealing eyes and whined to be released from the load he carried. Quickly Throw Stone knelt and untied the thong while Yodi hopped anxiously from one paw to the other.

"What is it, Yodi? Are The People at my cache? Don't hurt The People."

Already he knew it wasn't The People. Some animal had found his cache in the tree! All of his good meat—what had happened to it?

Free of the load, Yodi dashed toward the shelter. Throw

Stone heard an angry snarl. Then he saw the animal: dark brown and shaggy with a heavy body and short thick legs—a wolverine! It stood on its hind legs like a bear waiting for Yodi. Throw Stone hurled his spear at the animal, but the spear went skidding past. Yodi leapt at the wolverine and the two animals rolled over on the ground, snarling and scratching. Yodi bit into the wolverine's back and the animal broke free and dashed away with a lop-sided gallop.

"Come back, Yodi!" the boy called. "Leave him alone! Come back!" He watched the animals bound out of sight. Then he picked up his spear, listening as Yodi's yips faded in the distance.

Throw Stone walked back toward the shelter, wondering if Yodi could keep out of reach of the wolverine's long curved claws and heavy jaws. Maybe he could, for Yodi was the bigger of the two. The shelter and cache were wrecked. The wolverine had climbed the trees where the meat was hung, brought it down near the shelter, eaten what it wanted, and then sprayed the un-eaten meat with a terrible odor.

Throw Stone moved across the stream at the head of the lake. He found a tall tree where he could no longer smell the wrecked cache.

"I'll wait for Yodi," he told himself. He stacked his gear under the tree and built a fire. The weather was quite warm, but the sun had disappeared behind heavy dark clouds. From far away he heard thunder rolling.

"I won't build a shelter," he said aloud. He often talked to himself for the comfort of his own voice. "When Yodi returns, we'll go to the forest home."

He leaned against the tree and strained to hear Yodi's yipping, but all he heard was the rolling of thunder to the south.

"Yodi can follow the tracks to return. Or he'll see the fire. Yodi won't get lost. He's stronger and smarter than the wolverine. He won't let it kill him."

85

But he couldn't help thinking of the wolverine's long curved claws. He reached in his hunting pouch and folded his hand around the charm stone.

"Kill the wolverine. Bring back Yodi."

Water began to fall from the sky. Throw Stone looked up in surprise. What kind of magic was this? When there was thunder at the homeland by the sea, only snow or sleet came from the sky. But water falling from the sky? This was worse than snow! He had no covering except the scant shelter of the tree. He pulled the fur hood over his head, but the water beat at his face, ran down his clothing and into his skin boots. He was wet and cold. The fire smoked under the heavy wash of water and went out. The sky was black with clouds. He sat against the tree without moving, his teeth chattering while he waited for Yodi. He thought of his mother. How kind and calm she went about her work, and how secure he'd felt when he was with her. First he'd lost the Grandfather; then the Mother and the Grandmother were left behind, then his father had left him, and now Yodi was gone.

He tried to smile. "I wish I could leave me, too. But I'm always with me."

He thought of the stories the Grandmother and the Grandfather had told about the wolverines. Would they eat a boy? Yes, he thought so. Wolverines were believed to attack The People in the middle of the winter at the time of the fifth winter moon. But this was the second spring moon—almost summer. He had heard that wolverines would eat a downed and quivering animal before it was dead. If the wolverine killed Yodi and came back for him, what would he do?

He stared into the falling water, but all he saw was a porcupine calmly waddling along. That sticky animal had no reason ever to be afraid; he was armed with a body full of sharp needles.

At last the water stopped, but now it was dark. There was still

86

no sign of Yodi. Throw Stone built a fire. The damp wood smoked as it burned and made him cough. He ate some of the meat from his carrying bag, then crawled into his sleeping skin, still shivering.

The stars came out bright and fresh and soon the moon appeared. The water that had fallen from the sky turned to ice. The boy heard the hooting of an owl in a nearby tree, and the howl of a wolf in the white bark trees across the little lake. But he didn't hear the sound of Yodi.

He couldn't go to sleep and for no reason his heart was pounding hard. He raised up on his elbows.

"Danger," he said. "I feel danger."

Across the lake in the bright moonlight he saw the dark outlines of animals moving among the white bark trees toward the lake. What were they? Wolves? Yes—wolves.

"What can I do?" he said aloud. "I can't kill a wolf for that is evil magic. I know—I'll climb a tree!" As the wolves trotted closer, Throw Stone scrambled out of his sleeping skin and quickly examined the trees close by until he found one he could climb. He tied the carrying bag to a thong, climbed the tree and drew the bag up after him. He repeated this with the rest of the meat and gear. His heart was pounding hard, both from fear and hard work. Despite the cold he felt the perspiration run down his face. As he drew the last spear into the tree, he saw the wolves trot onto the frozen lake.

"Please, Yodi," he whispered, "Don't come back now. They will kill you. Stay away with your one wolverine. You can't fight a pack of wolves."

The wolves came closer. They were grey and carried their tails high. They looked almost like dogs as they leapt to the rocky shore and came toward him. At first it seemed the wolves might pass by without ever noticing the boy in the tree. Then one stopped and sniffed. Soon all were sniffing at Throw Stone's tree. Two of them rose, put their paws on the tree trunk and looked up.

What was this going to be? A game of waiting? Would the wolves keep him treed until his food gave out? They could do it. One or two could go off to hunt while the others stayed guarding the tree.

How had this terrible thing happened? He'd hated living at the forest home, so close to Acaba, but being treed by wolves was worse. Throw Stone kept his eyes on the wolves while one hand sought the charm stone. Again the magic worked!

The wolves turned to look at something else. Their ears perked forward and they snarled, showing their fangs. It was the little porcupine calmly passing by again.

"He's been out for a little walk," Throw Stone thought. "And now he's returning home."

One wolf moved close to the porcupine, then the other wolves circled him—tense, alert and snarling. The porcupine paused, moved out of the circle and waddled to a log and climbed onto it. The four snarling wolves followed behind cautiously. The little porcupine turned and arched his back, tucking his head safely between his front legs. Then he lashed sideways with his tail. Some of the needles shook loose from his tail and hit the closest wolf in the face. The wolf howled in pain, fought at the quills with his paw, then dashed off across the lake with his three companions following.

Throw Stone laughed aloud as he watched the little porcupine go on its way as calm as ever. "Thank you, my little sticky friend," he said, climbing out of the tree. "You saved my life."

He stacked more wood on the fire until it roared. "If wolves are afraid of fire, then I'll have the biggest fire that was ever made. It will be so big I'll roast myself."

He climbed the tree and threw down all his gear. The wolves

might come back, but he didn't think so. Anyway, he couldn't live in a tree forever.

"I'm no bird," he said. Then he remembered the berries in his hunting pouch. He ate a few and yawned.

"I'm tired," he said. "But I must build a shelter so the water from the sky won't fall on me. When the sun comes again, I shall try to find Yodi."

THE BIG VISITORS

Yodi's tracks

Wolverine tracks

THROW STONE awoke to bright sunlight. He ate some of the dried meat from his carrying bag and walked across the stream to the grassy lake shore. Here, thin ice had formed but below the surface he again saw the big silvery fish swimming lazily in the cold water. He tried to catch one with his hands, but missed.

"I don't really want you, fish. I have to be starving to want to eat you."

He returned to the tree shelter and removed his furs. The warm sun beat on his bare chest which was pale in contrast to his wind-browned face and hands. Then, with only his spear and hunting pouch, he set off to trail Yodi.

He found the water washed tracks of the two animals, but

90

couldn't tell which belonged to the wolverine, which to Yodi. Nor could he tell who was chasing or being chased. Finally, on a rocky patch of ground the tracks faded away. Unhappily the boy turned back toward the lake.

The frozen lake shimmered in the sunlight and the air was so clear he could see far in every direction. He stopped and sniffed. The wind blowing from the lake ruffled his hair. Bear smell! Close to the lake—bear smell. He crept along remaining as well hidden as he could.

He peeked out from a patch of junipers close to the rocky lake shore. On the opposite shore he saw two enormous shaggy brown bears.

"So that's what poor Dark Hunter had to face in the mountains!" he whispered. "I'm sure he and his family are dead. The bears are so big no two hunters could kill them as my father and I did the white bear." The bears coughed, grunted and sniffed.

The bears searched until they found a thin place in the ice where the fish had come close to the shore to feed. They reached in with their tremendous forepaws, pinned the lazy fish to the shallow bottom of the lake, and dipped their heads into the water to seize the fish in their teeth. They brought the fish to the grassy shore and gobbled them up. Three more bears joined the others on the river bank. They too dipped their heads in the water to catch the fish or splashed them out of the water with their great hairy paws. Throw Stone remained hidden in the cluster of juniper trees.

Instead of being afraid, Throw Stone enjoyed watching the bears. If he ever found The People again, the stories he'd have to tell!

"I'll be called Throw Stone, the Great Story Teller, for I've seen the big brown bears and I've been treed by a pack of wolves."

Watching the bears was more exciting than watching a meeting of The People with the dancing and singing. As the bears moved back and forth and slapped at the fish, the boy had to put his hand over his mouth to keep from laughing.

More bears came, by twos and threes, strolling along together like families out on a visit. Soon the entire grassy slope was filled with the brown beasts slapping at the silvery fish and dragging their catches to the shore. One bear dug for roots and ate them; another turned over a rotted log and ate the bugs under it. Two cubs jumped at each other, whining and rolling over and over in the grass. One nipped the other, and the bitten one dashed off and climbed a small tree. Throw Stone held his nose. If only the bears didn't smell so bad he might join them and become a bear, for they were having fun.

"They'd name me Little Skinny Bear With No Hair On My Hide."

He crawled back to the tree shelter and ate some of the dried meat. He was thirsty but afraid to go to the lake for a drink, so he sucked the ice-covered branches at his shelter. All through the trees he heard the crackling sound of ice falling. He swallowed the dry meat and ate a few of his precious berries. They only made him thirstier.

When the sun faded away and the cold night air hit him, he longed to build up his fire, but he dared not attract the bears.

"Don't bears ever sleep?" he wondered.

The moon came out and made the ice-covered lake bright and silvery. In the moonlight the bears weren't as friendly to each other. They prowled along the shore, snarling and fighting. Throw Stone's eyelids grew heavy. He snuggled down into his sleeping skin.

"I wish they'd go away. They smell bad and I'm thirsty."

When he awoke he listened for the bears. He heard nothing. He crept to the juniper trees and looked across the lake. The

92

bears were gone. The grey, grassy bank of the lake was torn by their rough paws and there was a smell of bear and fish. Throw Stone went to the rocky shore and found a place free of ice. He stretched himself on the ground like an animal and drank.

He filled his skin bag with water, and thought, "I won't get caught without water again." He looked at the sky. It was grey and full of snow clouds. Spring seemed to have vanished again.

"I must leave this place quickly," he said. "Before the bears return. The lake must be their home."

He loaded his gear. "Yodi isn't coming back. He's still trailing the wolverine or he's dead. What should I do? I can't wait at the lake where the bears live and I can't find my way through the mountains to Dark Hunter and his family. I could go back to the forest home but—" He shook his head. "No. The dream was magic. They must be dead."

He went in the direction Yodi and the wolverine had disappeared. He had to try to find Yodi even though he knew the trail disappeared on the rocky ground. He walked through the forest and along the ridge beside the stream that led back to the forest home. A light snow began to fall.

When he was beyond the place where he'd lost the tracks on the rocky ground, he guessed at the direction. The trees were beginning to thin and he decided the animal being chased—whether it was the wolverine or Yodi—would head for open space.

He wandered among the tall green trees sprinkled with fresh snow and when he could walk no more, built a fire and ate some meat. He was running out of food, but he was so eager to find Yodi he hadn't tried to hunt. While he walked, he'd seen rabbits and birds but not once had he thrown his spear.

"I'll be sorry later," he told himself. "But I must find Yodi."

He trudged forward, now searching, now giving up, now searching again. He was almost ready to give up and build another fire when his path crossed tracks. He studied them, so excited he could hardly keep from setting out in a run after them. Yes—there in the fresh snow were the tracks of the big-footed wolverine. And mingled with them were Yodi's! Yodi was chasing the wolverine!

"My grandfather helps me. My charm stone works," he said.

In the light snow covering he could easily follow the tracks. "You have big feet, wolverine, even though you aren't as big as my Yodi."

He followed the trail, full of wonder that he'd ever found it in the vast forest.

He grinned. "Even without my charm stone, it's in my blood to find my way."

Not far beyond, in the shadow of a tree, he saw a flattened mark in the snow where Yodi had sat. The wolverine's tracks ran to the tree. There were claw scratches in the bark. The wolverine had gone up the tree. Yes, Yodi had treed the wolverine!

Throw Stone looked up in the tree; nothing was there. Close to the place where Yodi had sat were four heavy marks which indicated that the wolverine must have jumped from the tree.

The boy shivered. "He tried to land on Yodi's back. My grandfather was right when he told long ago how the wolverine jumps from trees onto the backs of animals—and men."

He studied the tracks again. Yodi had been clever. He'd seen the wolverine's leap and dodged. The wolverine had taken off again with Yodi after him.

After a short distance the tracks became blurred and there were signs that the two animals had rolled and tumbled together in the snow. And there was a patch of blood. Throw Stone caught his breath.

"Please, please let it be the wolverine's blood."

Then the tracks shot off again. They were sprinkled with drops of blood.

THIN ICE

Caribou

AGAIN the tracks of the two animals led to a tree and again Throw Stone found the place where Yodi had sat alone. This time the dog had feasted, and the boy found the bones and four furred feet of a large rabbit. On the tree, he found scratches made of the wolverine's claws, but no blood. It was Yodi who was wounded!

"If he loses much blood, he'll be weak and the wolverine will kill him," thought the boy as he tried not to recall the old people's stories of the "Beast That Never Gets Enough Meat." So great, they said, was the wolverine's hunger that it was known to drive bears away from their kill. For a moment, Throw Stone wondered how Yodi had survived so long, but then he reminded himself that the dog was clever and fast and had jaws as strong as a wolf's. "I'd hate to have a dog like Yodi chasing me," he thought. But the drops of blood worried the boy.

Throw Stone walked as fast as he could, for now he felt he was catching up with the two animals. But when he rested he had no more dried meat. The berries were gone, too. He found three bird's eggs in a nest and ate them, then tightened his belt. Again and again he found signs that told of the wolverine's tree climbing and Yodi's waiting. At the base of one tree were the feathers of a white bird. The bird must have had a broken wing or Yodi could not have caught it while he kept the wolverine treed.

Finally Throw Stone came to a patch of snow splotched with blood so fresh that he shook in fright. Had the two animals finally fought it out? Was this Yodi's blood again or that of the wolverine? The answer couldn't be far away. Throw Stone was almost afraid to find out.

Then he heard Yodi's little yip. In the shadow of a tall green tree lay Yodi with a grin-like look on his face. Between his paws was the carcass of a large rabbit he had just killed. Above in the tree, the wolverine stretched limply on a branch that grew horizontally from the tree trunk. His large yellow eyes stared hungrily from his yellowish white face, and the coarse long hair that covered his skin seemed barely enough to hide his body and short bony legs.

Wagging his bushy tail, Yodi ran to Throw Stone. The dog's left shoulder was wounded. Here, the hair had been torn off exposing a raw slash. Throw Stone hugged the dog.

"My poor Yodi. I'll fix your shoulder." The boy picked up the rabbit and said, "Come with me, Yodi."

Yodi danced back and forth, looking up at the treed wolverine. Throw Stone laughed at him.

"Don't you think you've done enough to that poor wolverine? He may not have the strength to climb down out of the tree."

Nearby the boy built a fire, skinned the rabbit and he and the dog ate. He hung the rest of the rabbit meat in a tree. From a scrubby juniper tree he plucked leaves, mashed them and applied the leaves to Yodi's shoulder wound. He covered the wound with a piece of animal skin and tied the skin and leaves in place with a thong wrapped around Yodi's body. Yodi held very still for this treatment and licked Throw Stone's face whenever he got the chance.

"Quit," laughed Throw Stone. "If I wanted to clean myself I would rub off with snow. I don't need you to help me." He took out the charm stone. "Lick this." The dog obeyed him. "Now your shoulder will be like it was, except for a very handsome scar. It won't be as handsome as the scar on my father's face, but for a dog it will be very good."

They rested and went on toward the forest home. Again they slept in a tree shelter. The light of the sun woke Throw Stone. He stretched and smiled. "I have Yodi again and we have meat. We'll go back to the forest home. While I slept I had a new dream. I saw my father walking with the colored lights of the north behind him. I believe this dream is true. Perhaps my family is at the forest home."

He longed to see them again, to hear them talk. He missed their voices more than anything. "I wonder if they'll think I'm different?" He looked down at himself. He'd grown. Now his grandfather's loose trousers fit him better. He almost filled the fur top, too.

"I'm almost as big as my grandfather was," he said. "Though my grandfather wasn't very big. Still, my grandfather was a man, not a boy."

They returned to the forest home without trouble, hunting rabbits and birds along the way. His family was not there, and again Throw Stone wondered if they were gone forever.

Spear in hand, he walked to the big river. "Acaba, are you

there?" he called. "Let me see you! I saw the wolves and I was no longer afraid! I saw the bears and I didn't run! Perhaps if I see you, I'll throw my spear at you!" He saw nothing and while he shouted, Yodi sat looking at him curiously, his head cocked to one side.

The forest home was buried in the snow, but the cached meat was safe. Throw Stone was glad to be back, even though he was still alone. At least it was familiar country. He dug the snow away from the shelter.

"We're home, Yodi. I don't hear Acaba so perhaps he's gone away and let the sun rise high in the sky. Still, I don't know. There's much snow and ice and it should be gone if this is the Land Where the Sun Lives."

He tried not to think of the Father and the women. Which dream had been the magic one? Was his family dead like the broken tree limbs? Or were they walking with the northern lights behind them? The Father had said he would try to return during the winter. It was the last spring moon and the next moon would be summer. The Father had been gone for five moons.

The boy and dog killed another caribou. Although Throw Stone found fewer and fewer animals, he had not gone hungry.

One day, armed only with his thrusting spear and hunting pouch, he walked with Yodi along the river's edge; humming to himself and kicking at the snow. His right big toe poked out of his boot and was almost worn through the skin trousers underneath.

"My boots are worn out and I have no one to sew for me. I have no needle to do it myself nor do I know how. What shall I do when my feet are bare?"

He looked across the river and caught his breath. On the other shore he saw a strange animal. The color of it sent fear to his heart. The beast was red. Throw Stone clutched at his spear.

The beast appeared to be very small and the boy decided to venture out onto the frozen river for a closer look. Was it Acaba? And if so, was Acaba only a small animal no larger than his dog? Throw Stone and Yodi walked far out onto the slippery ice.

The farther they walked, the bigger the beast appeared, and yet they were still less than half way across the river! The beast, too, had left his shore and was coming toward them. It grew bigger and bigger. Red and hairy, it had a long snout, longer than any sea lion's the boy had ever seen. It had long tusks and flapping ears, and its hairy legs ended in big hairy pads. The animal was a giant and it was red. There was no mistake—this was Acaba!

But was it a red cloud? An evil spirit? Or was it just a beast— the biggest and most awful beast Throw Stone could imagine.

Acaba made a "poo-poo" sound, and with a slow, lumbering walk, he moved toward the boy; his long snout thrust out before him as if feeling and smelling for something.

Throw Stone stopped as the ice had begun to sway under him. When he and the dog stopped, the beast stopped, too, and stood absolutely still except for the long snout feeling in the air. Could the beast see him? It didn't act like it, and his eyes were set on the side of his head like a bird's. The wind was behind Throw Stone and Yodi, so Acaba must be *smelling* them and he saw them only when they moved.

Yodi whined and crowded at Throw Stone's legs. Acaba's big ears flopped forward at the sound.

"Be still, Yodi," said Throw Stone. He thought of throwing his spear, but the spear would only prick the beast, and then be lost. He remembered the rocks in his hunting pouch and took one out. Yodi growled and jumped forward. Again, the beast moved toward them. Acaba was only a short distance away when the ice under him began to give way. He stopped and backed a step.

Throw Stone stretched back with his rock and threw it as hard

103

as he could. The rock hit Acaba's snout. The beast let out a piercing squeal, sat back on his haunches like a dog, then rose slowly, his snout curled back over his head.

Throw Stone and the dog turned and ran. They didn't look back until they had reached the bank. When they turned to see, Acaba was disappearing into the trees across the river.

Shaking all over, Throw Stone went back to his fire. Acaba was across the river and would have charged them if the river ice hadn't been so thin. But what now? If the river should freeze solid, would Acaba come to kill him? Or if it melted altogether, might Acaba be able to swim the river? Now he knew why the animals had disappeared, even though the sun was high. Acaba had driven them away, just as his grandfather had told him.

Throw Stone packed his gear. "I was right to leave the forest home once before. We'll go away again. I found my way to the west; I can find my way to the north. I've lived alone so long and done so many things, I believe I'll soon be a man."

He loaded his carrying bag with meat and cached that which he couldn't carry. He rolled up the sleeping skin and tied it to Yodi's back. All the time he kept glancing toward the river, but Acaba was out of sight. Throw Stone and his dog headed toward the homeland.

At the top of the second ridge beyond the forest home, he stopped. He could hardly believe his eyes. Two figures, one behind the other, were moving slowly toward him. He shouted and waved, but the two people were burdened with loads on their backs and didn't look up nor wave. *Two.* It couldn't be his family because there would have been three people and a dog. But The People anyway. He waited, hardly able to contain his excitement.

THE DEADLY SUMMER

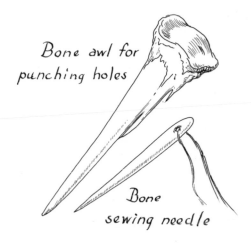

Bone awl for punching holes

Bone sewing needle

As THE TWO figures came closer, the one in front lifted his head. It was his father! Throw Stone ran to them—then he saw his mother. He embraced her and took the load from her back.

"My grandmother?" Throw Stone asked fearfully.

The Father shook his head. "She chose to stay behind in the homeland. She was too old for the long journey and she knew she might delay us until mid-summer. Then we could not cross the thawed streams."

"Did she go out in the snow to die like Grandfather?"

"No. She stayed in our home with a supply of meat. She was joyful I had found animals and that you and I were alive and safe. She was happy to stay there in the homeland. She said if

105

others of The People were still alive and came to the home, she would tell them of the Land Where the Sun Lives and where there are the animals. When we left her, she was singing one of the old songs."

At the mention of the Grandmother, the Mother wept.

"I won't ask any more questions about my grandmother," Throw Stone told himself. "It makes my mother cry. Now she has no other woman to talk to. She will be lonely."

"What of Dog That Bites?" asked the boy.

"He started with us on the journey," said the Father. "We were careful of the meat. I guess we did not give him enough for he began hunting on his own and soon he grew as wild and mean as a wolf and he disappeared. I believe he must have joined a wolf pack but I am not sure. We should have killed him at the homeland and left his meat for your grandmother. I see your dog has survived and done well. Where were you going, loaded in your gear?"

"We were going to search for you."

Throw Stone studied his father who had changed much. The Father now resembled the Grandfather, but without the brave look of the hunter which the Grandfather kept even as an old man. The Father had traveled to the homeland by the sea and returned to the forest home during six long moons. (A trip of twelve hundred miles.) The journeys had made an old man of him. There was a crease between his eyes, his lips were cracked and his face haggard, with skin hanging loose around his face scar.

"Father," said Throw Stone. "I've seen Acaba. He's across the big river so we mustn't return to the forest home. He's big as a mountain and red and woolly and he makes a terrible noise."

The Mother gasped and her eyes grew wide. The Father shook his head sadly; his shoulders were stooped. "We must rest. We must go to the forest home. I see you have meat with you. Is there still meat cached at the forest home?" The boy nodded.

"Please, Father," said Throw Stone. "I threw a rock at Acaba and he'll cross the river to kill me. Only the thin ice at the middle of the river saved me."

They had reached the ridge and the Father looked across the river. "I see nothing."

"Not now, but before you came—"

The Father shook his head and his lips quivered. "Perhaps you dreamed it."

"No! Yodi saw him, too!"

The Father moved toward the forest home. "We are very tired. We must have rest. I care for nothing but meat and rest."

They went to the forest home, and after they had rested, Throw Stone again said: "We must move, Father. Acaba has driven the animals away as Grandfather said he would. I *did* see him. It wasn't a dream."

"No," said the Father, "Even after we sleep many times, I cannot go on. I have traveled as far as I shall ever go. There are fish in the river. We will live on fish."

Just then Throw Stone heard Acaba's shriek come from across the river. "There! That's Acaba."

They walked to the clearing in the trees. "I see nothing," the Father said. "The forest is full of strange sounds. You only dreamed of Acaba, my son. We will stay."

Later, Throw Stone told the Father and the Mother of his search for Dark Hunter, of the bears, the wolves and the wolverine. He told how Acaba had looked like a small dog across the river, but had grown bigger and bigger, as Throw Stone and Yodi drew near him, until finally he was as big as a mountain. His mother listened with wide-eyed interest but his father seemed to be thinking of something else.

Throw Stone huddled in a corner of the shelter. "When my father is rested he will ask me to tell him the stories of the animals I've seen."

It was summer again. The sun shone clearly. Acaba had not sent any clouds since the Father and the Mother had returned. Except in sheltered places the snow was gone, and there were violet and purple flowers and green plants growing. The ice in the river had melted. Throw Stone and his family wore only their fur trousers. Even in these they perspired when the sun was high.

Throw Stone helped the Father spear fish along the shallow waters of the river. The boy shook his head sadly when he looked at his father.

"Is this my father or my grandfather?" he said. "Will he ever be rested and strong again?"

"What?" asked the Father.

Throw Stone bit at his tongue. He must remember not to talk to himself. He wasn't alone any more.

The boy hunted for the broad-tailed animal with the orange teeth that lived in the mound houses. Many moons ago, he'd been afraid to kill and eat a strange animal, but now he knew all meat was good. He'd traveled much and had seen almost every kind of animal being eaten by another. He found one of the broad-tailed animals chewing on a tree and he threw his spear and killed it.

Its fur was like the seal's and its meat was fat and tasty. Throw Stone cut the carcass into narrow strips and strung it alongside the fish that the Father had speared. The meat dried in the smoke from the fire.

A fire was kept burning continuously to drive mosquitoes away from the shelter. Always, wherever they had lived, there were mosquitoes in summer, but never so many as here. At night, they swarmed and buzzed over Throw Stone until he couldn't sleep. He would tuck his head under the furs to escape them, only to surrender and come out for air. Even Yodi, whining in the darkness, fought at the mosquitoes with his paws.

The Mother had brought along her sewing kit and she patched

Throw Stone's boots so that his big toe was no longer cold. She looked at the clothing he wore and frowned. His grandfather's old clothes were torn and cracked and the matted fur worn thin.

"You must have new clothes," said his mother. "Pick the skin you want."

After discussing it with his father, Throw Stone handed her the white bear skin. She softened the inside of the skin by soaking it with water and scraping it with a stone scraper, and by jerking it back and forth between her knuckles. With a knife she cut out pieces for the front and back of the coat, the front and back of the trousers. Then, running a long piece of finely cut sinew through the hole of a long narrow bone needle, she laced the front and back of each part together. She fashioned a hood and attached it to the coat in the same way.

Throw Stone put on the new clothing.

"How fine you look!" said the Mother. "Like a brave hunter."

Throw Stone laughed. "More like a white bear. I hope my father doesn't spear me."

Besides sewing, the Mother tended the fire and cleaned the fish. She didn't complain about having to eat mostly fish nor did she complain about the mosquitoes that swarmed around her even more than around the Father or boy. Without grumbling she stayed where the Father was. She did what the Father wanted.

Soon they had eaten all the red meat except for the thin dry strips peeled from the skin of the broad-tailed animal. Throw Stone could find no other animals to kill. All that was left were the fish he and the Father speared.

Summer passed and it was the first winter moon again—thirteen moons since Throw Stone had left the homeland. Already he found it hard to remember his old home. It was like a dream that comes and goes. The sun was still high in the sky, dim behind the snowy clouds that Acaba sent from across the river. The violet and purple flowers had died; yellow flowers took

111

their place only to freeze, shrivel and turn black. There were no more green plants nor any animals in the forest. Even the black ravens had gone.

All through the summer Throw Stone had begged his father to move on, to go away from the shriek of Acaba and the droves of mosquitoes. He hated the taste of fish. Yodi, who had once choked on a fish bone, picked at his food cautiously, his ears perked forward as if he disapproved of fish altogether.

The boy and the dog went to the river where the broad-tailed animals had lived. The little mound houses were still there, but weathered.

"It's been a long time since we've seen one of them," Throw Stone told Yodi. "Their houses aren't well-cared for anymore. Are they gone? We shall see. It's our last chance for meat." Throw Stone sat and waited patiently until the sun disappeared.

"They're gone," he said. "Like the other animals, Acaba has driven them away."

They returned to the shelter.

Throw Stone joined the Father and Mother in a meal of fish and then, surprising even himself, he turned to the Father and said, "Since you came back from the homeland we have stayed here. Now, the summer is gone and it is the beginning of the first winter moon. I am leaving."

"Yodi and I will go south and find where the animals live. Then you will leave this place of Acaba where there is nothing to eat but fish."

The Father shook his head like an old man. "Go if you wish."

Throw Stone wasn't sure, but he thought he saw his mother smile.

JOURNEY SOUTH

Throw Stone's tracks

Mastodon tracks

LOADED WITH his pack and some dry fish, Throw Stone and the dog set out southward. Not long after they started, the boy found a fallen tree which had been stripped of leaves and bark by rabbits.

"We're in luck!" he cried. "The rabbits have been feeding here. We'll have meat."

Against trees and under bushes, Yodi found brown rabbits that lay hidden flat on the ground. Throw Stone speared them. They were just as big as snow rabbits and tasted better.

"What would I do without you?" the boy asked Yodi. The dog howled for an answer.

As soon as they had rabbit meat, Throw Stone threw away the fish. But, he knew that if he traveled very far, he'd need more than rabbit meat to keep strong.

"I'll hunt for the large animals that used to live at the forest home," he told Yodi.

Throw Stone walked far and slept many times rolled in his sleeping skin beside a fire.

Once he saw wisps of smoke rising into the murky sky ahead of him. His pace quickened. "Are The People there? Look, Yodi, the smoke from many fires. Perhaps many of The People from the homeland have reached here first! We'll have a joyful meeting."

The country before them was a rolling, rocky land with brown shrubs and patches of dirty snow. The boy kept his eyes on the streams of smoke. Near them, he climbed a hill. Below was a burned, black valley. The trees were charred and burned to stumps. A few still smouldered.

Throw Stone shook his head sadly. "That makes the smoke, Yodi. The People aren't here. I'm the first."

They descended into the black valley. "How did this happen? None of The People were here to start a fire. Can a fire start without The People?" He walked across the sooty land with ashes floating on the wind.

"Yes, I guess there was fire before there were The People." He'd never thought of it before, always supposing The People created this magic.

"See, Yodi? The fire came alone to this valley and burned it black."

They walked through the valley and up a hill. Beyond, the land was unburned. Black ravens flew low overhead and a caribou raced in the distance. Throw Stone was happy again.

"When I went to the mountains searching for Dark Hunter, I was afraid of animals and afraid I'd get lost. Now I'm not afraid when I'm alone. I like to travel with you, Yodi. The whole country is ours and I can shout and do whatever I like without fearing my father's frowns. There are few mosquitoes here." Then he laughed. "And *no* fish. If there are fish in the stream, scare them away so I won't be tempted to catch them."

Yodi yipped and wagged his tail. "I think you're learning to talk. Or maybe now I can understand dog talk. You're saying: 'No more fish.' "

Together they killed a young caribou that had strayed from the herd. Now they had good red meat. They cached the rabbit meat in a tall tree together with the caribou meat they couldn't carry. Remembering the wolverine, Throw Stone piled brushy limbs around the tree trunk.

When they had traveled far (fifty miles) the trees became different from both those of the forest home and those that grew toward the mountains. There were still some of the white bark trees and the tall green ones. But there were others with broad leaves that were red and yellow like flowers.

The travelers found many streams with cold, fast-running water like the big river by the home in the forest, but these streams could be crossed by wading where there were rocks.

Finally they came to a river neither as wide as the big river nor as shallow as the streams they had crossed. The green water ran fast with tumbling waves. Throw Stone looked at the sky. The sun peeped from behind swift moving dark clouds; there was no hazy mist like that at the forest home. Throw Stone and Yodi climbed a high rock.

As they climbed, Throw Stone saw jagged, snow-covered mountains to the west; a dark forest to the east. He turned around to look across the river. He saw a broad, rolling country covered with tall green grass and feeding on the grass were animals, four abreast, that trailed as far as he could see!

They were similar to the musk ox, but bigger and with longer

115

horns. Each animal had a high hump on his shoulders, a long beard, and shaggy hair around its forelegs. The body hair was brown, the face hair black. They made a great grunting sound as they fed, and their horns clattered together. This was indeed where the animals lived, just as his grandfather had told him! They had found what they were looking for. (They had walked over one hundred miles since they had left the forest home.)

Throw Stone shouted for joy and threw rocks into the river to celebrate his discovery. And Yodi chased his tail in the excitement. The animals looked up from their feeding and moved a few steps closer to the river.

"They're curious," said Throw Stone. "They've never seen one of The People before."

He slid down the rock, the dog at his heels. "I'll go over there." He ran to the river's edge, then stared at the tumbling white waves. He couldn't see the bottom. He stripped off his boots and his clothing down to the skin pants and he stepped into the icy waters. The river bottom sloped downward and was covered with small rocks and gravel. Three more steps and he was in water up to his arm pits and the swiftness of the waters threatened to turn him over. He threw out his arms to balance himself, afraid to move forward or backward.

"Yodi!" he called to the dog watching from the bank.

Yodi plunged into the waters and paddled over to him, head held high. Throw Stone clutched at a handful of fur on Yodi's back and held on. The dog paddled back to shore, balancing the boy.

Shivering, Throw Stone built a big fire at the foot of the rock he'd climbed.

"I still do many foolish things," he told the dog. "In my eagerness I tried to cross the river at the worst place. I should have searched the length of the river for a shallow spot."

After he was dry and dressed, he explored the rocky banks.

Half hidden behind a growth of low shrubs was an opening.

"We could sleep in there, Yodi. Then I wouldn't have to build a shelter. I hope it doesn't belong to a bear."

He found a big stick and made a torch of it by holding one end in the fire until it flamed. Then cautiously he crept inside the rock opening. He found nothing but a stack of bones.

"Some animal has slept here and some other animal came in and killed him." Throw Stone dragged tree limbs inside the rock opening and started a fire, half expecting something to pop out of the rocks.

"When I wake up again I want to see if I only dreamed about all those animals."

Streaks of lightning cut the darkening sky and a loud crackle of thunder followed. Curious to see how the big animals would act when it stormed, Throw Stone scrambled outside while Yodi stayed in the shelter of the rocks. The wind was blowing hard. He climbed up the big rock and balanced himself to keep from being blown off his feet.

The big animals had moved into a compact mass, their short tails up. They were uneasy—snorting and pawing the earth. A few ran a short distance, then returned to the herd. There was another flash of lightning followed by a loud crackle of thunder. The herd of big animals broke into a gallop and disappeared over a hill.

When Throw Stone returned to the rock shelter, Yodi was cringing against the wall and whining.

"You're as big a coward as the new animals I've found. The water has begun to fall from the sky but it can't get you here. When the sun comes again we'll return to the forest home to tell my father about the new animals."

But Yodi could not be cheered. He lay against the wall and put both paws over his nose.

When the sun rose, Throw Stone left the rock shelter. The

117

ground was soggy and slippery with mud. He climbed the big rock and saw that the animals had returned to feed on the grass. He followed the river's course until he found a place where he could clearly see the bottom.

"I'll bring my father and my mother. We'll cross into the new land right here." They started back to the forest home.

After two sleeps, the cold wind struck while they struggled across a ridge. The boy patted the shivering Yodi.

"We're getting back to the land of Acaba. See how he sends the cold wind to torment us." Throw Stone's eyes watered, his nose ran, and each time he took a breath of the cold air, his chest ached. His fingers and toes felt swollen and stiff with cold. He tried to walk backward to keep the strong wind out of his face, but he stumbled over a log and fell. After that he walked with one arm across his face to shield it, but still he was in agony. It began to snow—a hard driving snow—and they leaned into the strong wind and fought their way back toward the forest home.

They found the place where they had cached the caribou and rabbit meat. After they slept, they moved on, carrying with them a part of the meat. The rest was left until they returned with the Father and the Mother.

By the time they reached the small stream back of the forest home, Throw Stone's stomach hurt from hunger. The meat they had carried was gone.

"We'll be glad to eat some of my father's fish," he told Yodi. The snow was deep—so deep they were wading instead of walking. When they started across the frozen stream with snow covering its icy surface, the dog turned west toward the mountains and whined.

"You want to go back to where you found the wolverine, Yodi? Do you think that is a better place to live than where we eat fish and hear Acaba's shriek? I think so, too, but now we've found an even better place where the animals live in the south. We must tell my father and mother."

Throw Stone struggled up the slope eager to see his family. He'd been away for most of the first winter moon. Yodi came slinking after him. The snow thinned as they climbed to the top of the ridge.

Here Throw Stone stopped and stared in amazement. Had he somehow come the wrong way? The forest home was gone! In place of the shelter there were splinters of broken limbs covered with snow. All was silent. There were no tracks of anything. Yodi crowded close to him.

Throw Stone cleared away the snow until he found a patch of earth. *His heart sank*. He saw big round tracks pressed deep into the hard dirt. Acaba! It must be Acaba. Had Acaba come before the snow fell—when there was only water in the river? Could Acaba swim like the seal and the walrus and like the broad-tailed animals? Or could he fly like the birds? What had he done with the Mother and the Father? Had he carried them away? Was he truly an evil spirit and had he made them disappear?

He searched the broken limbs that had been the shelter, but all that he found was one small piece of fur skin no larger than a child's hand.

"Father!" he cried. "Mother!"

He held Yodi close to him and wondered what he should do next. Then he climbed a tall tree to look for some sign of his family. There was nothing. No—wait. Far beyond the wreckage of the shelter were fresh tracks in the snow; the big round tracks of Acaba! The beast had destroyed the home long before but now he'd returned. Was he looking for Throw Stone who had struck him with a rock? The boy scrambled out of the tree. He ran to the tracks and studied them. The tracks overlapped each other in the line of path. How could such a great beast make so narrow a trail?

Throw Stone untied the roll of skin on Yodi's back. He raised his spear and shook it. "I will follow you, Acaba, and kill you!"

With Yodi at his heels, Throw Stone plunged forward, following the tracks that led through the trees down toward the river.

THE WIDE TRAIL

Binding the spear-head to the shaft

As Throw Stone and his dog followed Acaba's tracks, the boy wondered if he were the only remaining one of The People.

"And perhaps I won't live long," he told the dog. "For I'll fight Acaba until I kill him or he kills me."

Where the trail led down the slope to the river, the snow deepened. The heavy beast made a path as it ploughed through the deep snow banks, but Acaba's body was so high and his legs so long, he didn't clear a path for the boy and dog. Rather he churned up the soft snow and made following more difficult. At the boy's side, Yodi leapt through the soft snow that sometimes came up to his neck. Once, he disappeared under the snow and Throw Stone had to dig him out.

"My legs are as weak as twigs from having to wade through this snow," he told the dog. "But we must go on."

He stumbled across broken tree limbs and small trees which Acaba had yanked up by the roots.

"Look, Yodi. This is what Acaba eats—leaves. He likes the tender green leaves at the top so he pulls up the whole tree. And look at the bushes. He's eaten them, too. Wait. Listen." He heard a strange swishing sound. "That's Acaba. He makes many noises."

Sometimes Throw Stone drew so close to Acaba he could hear the loud rumbling noises of the beast's stomach as he fed. Then Throw Stone and Yodi would try to catch him by ploughing through the deep snow as fast as they could go. But Acaba disappeared, completely and silently. Even the stomach noises stopped. Again they followed the path stripped bare of vegetation.

"How much he eats!" said Throw Stone to Yodi. "He will eat up the whole forest. Is he an evil spirit or just a hungry animal?"

The trail led north, close to the river, and once the path led onto the ice along the shore. Here, there were three large holes, now covered with thin ice, showing how the animal had ventured onto the river only to go back when the ice had given away.

The trail turned and headed west. The snow thinned and the ground was blown bare in spots by the wind. Throw Stone made a small fire and rested.

"The trail will be easier now," he told the dog. "The deep snow saved Acaba back at the forest home, but we'll catch him now." He tried not to think about what he would do with the beast when he *did* catch him. "But I must think of something," he told himself.

122

Yodi whined and put a paw over his nose. "I know," said Throw Stone. "You're hungry. So am I." He opened the hunting pouch. "See? We have nothing."

When they took up the trail again, it was harder than ever to follow Acaba. Had the wind changed and did the beast know that he was being followed?

At times Acaba walked carefully, making almost no mark on the ground, not touching a bush or tree. Once, over a hard rocky area, Throw Stone lost the trail completely! But Yodi sniffed around and they again picked up the trail. When Throw Stone was upwind of Acaba even *he* could follow by the sweet odor of mashed leaves and tree limbs.

Sometimes the beast seemed to go at a jog-trot endlessly, and it was then that he drew far ahead of Throw Stone.

Finally the trail circled and turned back toward the river again. Yodi refused to go on. He whined, crouched down and crawled along the ground, headed in the opposite direction. Throw Stone walked a little farther, then turned back impatiently.

"Yodi! Come on!" Yodi whined and continued to crawl away. "You're a bad dog," said Throw Stone. "You're making me fall farther behind Acaba."

Yodi tucked his head low and continued to creep away from Throw Stone. Angrily, the boy tied a leather thong around the dog's neck and dragged him until finally Yodi walked along, still tied.

The trail led back to the highest ridge where the forest home had been and followed alongside the little ice-covered stream.

"We're back where we started," said Throw Stone. The sun was gone and he couldn't see to follow the trail. He led the dog to where the forest home had been and untied him. Yodi ran away in the direction of the mountains again. Throw Stone coaxed him back and tied him to a tree.

"You're a bad dog, Yodi. I may leave you tied here while I hunt Acaba. I can't be running after you and trailing the beast at the same time."

Having eaten nothing since the last sleep, Throw Stone's stomach felt like it was in knots. At times he couldn't see clearly. He built a shelter and fire and covered himself with his sleeping skin. He slept fitfully and dreamed that Acaba speared him with one of his tusks and tossed him into the trees, where the yellow-eyed wolverine waited.

When the sun was up, Throw Stone searched the ground for rabbit tracks and the sky for birds. He must have something to eat! But he saw nothing—nothing but snow, ice and trees. He went to the wrecked cache and dug with a stick until he scratched up the Father's fish supply that had been mashed into the ground by Acaba. He tried to eat a bite of it, but the dirt tasted terrible. He gave it to Yodi who was still tied and the dog gobbled it up.

"How would you like a big piece of Acaba to eat, Yodi?" said the boy. "You stay here and I'll go get it for you."

Throw Stone wiped at his face, discouraged. How could a boy kill so big an animal? Acaba stood at least three times as tall as he was. Even to kill the white bear, which was not big at all by comparison, it had taken two hunters, two spears.

"I can't even reach a place to kill him," he said. Then he stood up, shocked. "No, but I can *throw*." He could use his sling and throwing spear. But what would the effect of one bone point be? It would wound, but not kill. Then, afterwards, how could Throw Stone escape the wounded Acaba? He wiped at his face again. This was a very big problem and he was only a boy.

"Not the sling. My hand spear. I'll attach the bone point tight to the spear shaft. If we are near brush when I strike at him, perhaps the spear shaft will hang in Acaba and catch in the brush. Then I can get away. I'll try for the chest."

With sinew, he firmly bound the bone point to the spear shaft.

124

"If I miss," he said, "then it's too bad for me." Yodi whined and tried to pull away from the tree. "No, stay there, bad dog. If I never come back, you can free yourself by chewing the thong like you did in the homeland. Go join Dog That Bites and the wolves. At least you'll have something to eat."

The trail led to the big river, turned south and followed along clumps of willows which lined the shore. The willows were banked high in snow. Thick ice was forming along the edge of the river, its slippery surface swept clean by the wind. Beyond, toward the other bank, deep water ran black under the grey sky.

Throw Stone couldn't hear Acaba nor could he smell him, because the wind was blowing from behind the boy. He was close, though, very close. Acaba's deep tracks cut all the way through the snow and in them the small plants were still moving and trying to straighten up. Acaba must have just passed!

"I've caught him," said Throw Stone licking his lips uneasily. "I feel as weak as a baby bird but I'll fight the great evil spirit, Acaba." He stopped and tested the wind. "The wind is in favor of the beast. Perhaps my grandfather was right. Perhaps Acaba controls the wind."

Behind a patch of brush, Throw Stone saw color; a reddish blur. He broke through and there was Acaba, facing him!

Acaba stood motionless except for his big ears that flapped backward and forward. His long snout waved back and forth before him, close to the ground. The beast made the soft "poo-poo-poo-poo" sound, then threw back his trunk and charged! Throw Stone raised his spear and held his ground.

"I can't turn and run. He'll catch me. Hang on! Hang on!" he told himself. The mountain of red hair and flesh descended on him, shrieking like the wind. Throw Stone waited as long as he could stand it, then threw the spear with all his might. It stuck high in Acaba's chest. Blood spurted from around the spear. The beast squealed and sat back on his haunches.

127

In that instant Throw Stone dashed into the brush. The roaring Acaba came after him, tearing and pounding through the brush. Throw Stone hurled himself under a clump of junipers. He felt like his heart was pounding in his mouth. He thrust his hand into the hunting pouch and clutched the charm stone.

"Please! Please!"

Then he breathed a little easier. The wind was now in his favor, Acaba couldn't smell him. As yet the beast hadn't seen him in the white bear skin clothing. It blended with the snow. Perhaps Acaba wouldn't find him—

The roaring beast thrashed through the brush close by, looking for the boy who lay still, holding his arm over his dark eyes to hide them, as the white bear had done long ago.

FIRE DANCE

Mastodon

ACABA did not find Throw Stone as he lay hidden in the junipers, but the boy could hear him roaring and charging among the trees and brush close to the river.

"One bone point won't kill him," said Throw Stone. "Unless he bleeds to death." What to do? He *had* to kill Acaba for taking away his father and mother!

Throw Stone rolled out from under the junipers and ran back to the forest home where Yodi strained against the thong.

"All right, Yodi," he said unfastening him. "But don't run away. I need you. This is the biggest hunt *any* of The People ever had."

He grabbed his sling and spears and headed back to the raging beast. He found the tracks and he found blood. When the tracks led through brush, there was even more blood.

"Look, Yodi," Throw Stone whispered. "The spear shaft catches on the brush and tears open the wound in his chest."

Somewhere near, Acaba stood hidden. Throw Stone's heart pounded. A wounded animal was twice as dangerous. There was no sound now except the boy's breathing and the sound he made as he pushed through the snow. Behind the next clump of willows he might find Acaba. He stopped, and Yodi caught up with him. The bloody trail of Acaba was so crisscrossed Throw Stone could not follow it. He felt very weak.

"Where is he, Yodi? Find Acaba."

Head lowered, the dog moved slowly toward a dense growth of willows bordering the river. Throw Stone followed. He could not see beyond the edge of the trees. He crept slowly forward and carefully pushed back a tree branch.

There stood Acaba; the spear still stuck in his chest. He was bleeding badly but he was alive. He would still be able to charge.

Throw Stone crawled out of the trees and faced Acaba once more. They stared at each other and Acaba waved his long snout back and forth. Then the beast shrieked and charged. Throw Stone whirled his sling, threw a spear and missed! Terrified, he turned and ran. Then he felt Acaba's long snout start to wrap around his body. He screamed. Yodi, snarling, leapt at the snout and bit. Acaba released Throw Stone and squatted on his haunches. The boy rolled under a bush out of the way. Yodi growled and jumped in front of Acaba, as the squealing beast arose.

Running and howling, Yodi led Acaba onto the river ice. The boy rolled free of the bush and ran after them, shouting. Suddenly the beast stopped and started toward Throw Stone again.

The boy whirled and ran the other way. He could feel the river ice sway beneath him. He stumbled and fell to his knees.

Now Acaba was a great shadow standing on hind legs towering above the boy. On hands and knees, Throw Stone scrambled away toward the shore. Acaba's great woolly front pads crashed down and opened a yawning crack in the ice.

The boy and dog stood watching from the shore as the ice cracked all around Acaba's huge body. The beast fought to gain a foothold on the broken ice as the blood from his wound turned the water red. But slowly his body sank deeper and deeper until the swift running water upended him. His four woolly pads appeared for a moment above the surface, then the swift running water swept him away.

Throw Stone straightened up. "It is finished. I have killed Acaba." He dug into his hunting pouch and touched the charm stone. "Thank you, Grandfather. Everything you said has come true."

He and the dog climbed the slope to the old forest home. Again Yodi whined and started toward the mountains.

"Now I'll follow you," said Throw Stone. "I never want to see this place again."

The boy slowly pulled himself forward with each step; the dog leading the way and waiting for him to catch up. Everything seemed to be dim and blurred to Throw Stone and his head felt light.

"I haven't eaten in so long," he said. He followed the dog toward the mountains as long as he could, then fell to his knees.

"I can't go any farther." On hands and knees he crawled under the low branches of a tree burdened with snow. Yodi licked at his face and the boy tried to put his arm around the dog's neck, but he lacked the strength to do it.

"Find The People—" he said to the dog. Then he slumped forward and everything turned hazy and peaceful.

Throw Stone awoke and, at first, thought he was dreaming.

He saw his father and mother kneeling over him. But this couldn't be true! They'd been carried away by Acaba.

"Son," he heard, and it was his father's voice. He sat up and looked around. He was in a shelter similar to the forest home. Nearby was his mother. From the shelter opening he could see that outside by the fire were others; Dark Hunter, Dark Hunter's wife, Strong Girl, Silent Tongue and a woman with a girl child, neither of whom he'd ever seen before. He laughed with joy because now he knew he wasn't dreaming. He was alive, his family was alive, and Dark Hunter's family was alive! His mother held him in her arms as she had when he was a child, but after a glance from the Father, she released him.

"What happened?" asked Throw Stone. "I thought Acaba had destroyed you."

The Father shook his head. "I did not believe you when you said the great beast was across the river. But when you went away, the sound of him grew louder. When I was fishing, I saw him. Small he looked from that distance but you said he looked only the size of a dog across the river. Acaba started into the running waters of the river—the water is not deep in some places so he walked and then he swam. And he kept coming and getting bigger and bigger, just as you said. We could hear Acaba crushing the trees as he came toward the home."

Throw Stone saw that The People were crowding in the entrance to the shelter now that he was awake.

The Father continued, "I and your mother grabbed what we could and we ran away into the trees and hid. We fled toward the mountains until we could run no more. Then we came upon Dark Hunter and his family. We were exhausted and hungry. They took care of us."

"But how did you find me? I remember falling under a tree, but nothing else."

132

"We were preparing to set out to search for you," said the Father, "when Yodi found us."

"Yodi!" cried Throw Stone. "Where is Yodi?"

Dark Hunter smiled and pointed outside where Yodi romped with a small white dog. "The dog belongs to the new woman you see."

Throw Stone shook his head. "Yodi knew all along that you were here. He tried to lead me to you while I hunted Acaba."

"Acaba," said the Father. "You saw Acaba?"

"Yes," said Throw Stone. "I saw him and I killed him." The People gasped and moved closer.

The Father said, "You, a boy, killed Acaba?"

"I wounded him with my spear. He almost bled to death. Then Yodi led him to the river ice. Acaba chased me but his great body fell through the ice into the swift water. Acaba was nothing but an animal."

Dark Hunter said, "You killed him alone! You are now the greatest hunter of The People and your name should be Great Hunter."

"I should like to be called Great Hunter," said the boy.

"Now you *are* Great Hunter!" shouted Dark Hunter and the others agreed.

The boy ate the good dry red meat Dark Hunter provided. He saw Strong Girl staring at him like she used to do in the homeland. But now he didn't mind because she was staring as if to say, "You are Great Hunter."

Perhaps he would kill an animal for her and she could cut the hide and make new clothing for herself.

As Throw Stone rested, he listened to Dark Hunter's story.

"We followed the mountain way but the brown bears were greater than we," said Dark Hunter, wiping his face which was wet with perspiration. "You see there the wife of Silent Tongue

133

and the girl child? The wife was once wife of Big Fire Maker. The child is Big Fire Maker's child. There were four others with them. We joined them in the mountains where they, too, had come from the homeland. One night the brown bears stole into our camp and carried away Big Fire Maker and the four others. We fought but we could kill none of the bears and we were afraid they would come back. So we left the mountains and followed the stream to here."

The boy said, "And first my father and mother found you, and then Yodi found you. Are we far from the forest home?"

Dark Hunter replied, "No, not far." (They were, indeed, only about five miles away.) Dark Hunter raised his hand. "Now this will be our home, for with Acaba dead, the animals will return."

"No," said Great Hunter who a sleep ago had been a boy named Throw Stone. "My grandfather spoke of a land to the south, the Land Where the Sun Lives. Before I killed Acaba I found this land. Many big animals feed on tall grass there. I'll lead you to them."

The Father said, "Tell us of the big animals."

Throw Stone who was now Great Hunter told of his journey to the south and the animals that were like the musk ox, only bigger.

Then Dark Hunter said, "Lead us to the animals in the new land." All The People shouted and clapped their hands in joy.

Later Dark Hunter said, "Tell us of the wolverine, of the wolves and of the bears."

The boy smiled his big toothy grin and everyone smiled back at him. So they wanted him to be a story teller!

The People moved close to him, their eyes big, their mouths half open while he told the stories, making them even better than they really were. Strong Girl giggled in excitement.

When he stopped the stories, The People cried, "More! More!"

The Father held up his hand. "Now is the time for The Peo-

ple to make the big happy noise, for we will follow my son to the south to hunt the big animals." He began to chant,

"Great Hunter has killed the black musk ox
Great Hunter has killed the white rabbit and the brown
Great Hunter has killed the tan caribou
Great Hunter has trailed the wolverine
Great Hunter has seen the brown bears play
Great Hunter has killed Acaba, the red woolly beast."
As the Father sang, Dark Hunter joined in the refrain,
"Great Hunter has found the big animals in the Land Where
    the Sun Lives
Great Hunter will show us the way."

Silent Tongue joined in clapping his hands and stamping his feet, along with the three women and the young girl and child. The People formed a circle around the blazing fire.

Outside the circle of dancers, Yodi and the white dog romped.

At the head of the circling dancers was Throw Stone, the boy, his spear sling hanging from his neck for now he was Great Hunter. He would lead The People to the big animals in the new land.

The end.

APPENDIX

THE ICE AGE—25,000 YEARS AGO

TODAY the MacKenzie River flows slowly northward in a broad shallow stream which empties into the Arctic Ocean. Many channels pass through the flat treeless tundra where nothing grows except mosses, lichens and low shrubby sedges. The country bordering the Arctic Ocean is mostly barren, rocky land. Only during the short summer months when the sun shines most of the time do plants grow. The rest of the year the sun is seldom seen and the dark, cold land is usually blanketed by snow.

South of the Arctic Circle are stunted willows and aspen as well as cone bearing trees such as larch or tamarack, spruce and fir. All

138

these furnish food for many species of wild life. Farther south are trees which are bare of leaves in the wintertime—aspen, birch and ash, and along the stream banks—alders and willows.

Still farther south, grass-covered prairie reaches into the northland from the great plains.

At the time of this story, the mountain route and the route by way of the MacKenzie Valley were different than they are today. The weather was colder, the rivers and streams were different and even the valleys had a different shape.

25,000 years ago—as geologists and other scientists have reckoned time—the Ice Age was still in existence. Parts of Europe and America that were near the Arctic Ocean and some of the higher mountains throughout the world, as well as the Anarctic regions, were covered with ice. The western part of the Arctic Ocean, however, was ice free.

During this Ice Age, much of the ocean water was frozen into ice caps called glaciers. A glacier was formed by snow piling up year after year and freezing into hard clear ice. (The snow, of course, was frozen moisture that came from the oceans.) When the snow piled high on a glacier and turned to ice, its weight caused the glacier to move very slowly. It carried with it all the trash that had been washed onto it. When a glacier moved, it pushed and rearranged everything in its path. Mountain valleys were reshaped by the moving ice. Sometimes lake basins such as the Great Lakes were gouged out. Other times the great loads of rocks and gravel it carried were deposited by a melting glacier. If a glacier reached the sea, pieces of it would break away and great mountains of ice would float to sea as icebergs.

Because so much ocean water was drawn up and frozen into these ice caps, ocean levels were lower than they are today. As the water receded, a land bridge was left between Asia and America. Animals and men passed back and forth over the land bridge.

139

And, eventually, they moved south into much of North and South America. Later, these ice-free passages were covered by glaciers which remained for thousands of years until finally the ice began to melt. Today the only glaciers left are near the North and South poles and in some of the higher mountains.

25,000 years ago, during the time of this story, the Arctic seasons may have been like they are now. There was a long, dark winter from October to March, when the sun was either near the horizon or out of sight. Beginning in March, the sun climbed higher until it reached its peak in June and there was a time of continuous daylight during which the sun dipped below the horizon only a few hours each day. Then the short Arctic summer began, or, if it were delayed, there was only a month or so of strong sunlight during July or August. The plants blossomed (some from buds that were started the summer before). Only in the summer was there enough light and warmth for the few top inches of soil to thaw so the plants could mature. Below the top soil, the land remained frozen.

The plants furnished food for many of the animals—some kinds that live today and some that are now extinct such as the red, woolly mastodon (one genus of the elephant family) and the giant beaver. The sea animals, too, depended upon the sun to produce their food.

Many of the ways in which the people of the Arctic did things seem strange to us. Yet, they were the best possible ways those things could have been done. They had to be good or the people would not have survived. The materials they used: stones; and animal bones, skins, and sinew (muscle) were the best materials available for Arctic living.

Raw meat, which they preserved by quick freezing, gave the Arctic dwellers the greatest body-building ingredients. Animal heart, liver and other insides were especially rich in vitamins. (The liver of the white bear was too rich in vitamins—it was poisonous.) These people had nothing to eat except meat and fat, yet they survived and were probably healthy.

They knew the seasons of the year and measured time by the moon. The positions of the stars served as guides over snow-covered wastes that lacked landmarks.

Primitive people must have measured differently than we do today. Small things might have been measured by comparing to a finger, a hand, or an arm (just as our measurements originated). For longer measurements, there was a spear, as long as a man was tall. Beyond that, how could primitive man reckon? Likely he had no need for measuring distance unless he wanted to find out how far away some place was from his home. That could have been measured by how long it required to get there by walking. But walking how? On bare ground? Snowshoes? Ploughing through loose snow? Each would have been different. He could have measured distance by how far he could see another man on ice (10 miles), or many different ways. We have used such a device in this story so that the reader can compare our "miles" to the distance the boy and the father travel.

Our story has depended largely for its background on information others have gathered and published. This has been adapted to our own knowledge and experience to reconstruct the past: for example, the snowhouse we describe is from *The Friendly Arctic*, by V. Stefansson, published by the Macmillan Company. The use of the snowhouse and some of the other things described in our story are known only from what people living in the Arctic have used.

The people of our story—the first Americans—had their ancestry in the Old World. So we must look there for the archaeological background as nothing is known from the Arctic of the archaeology of 25,000 years ago. Only farther south in America have archaeologists found the implements of the early inhabitants of the land.

141

In telling our story we have not attempted to show the source for each part of it, but this is our acknowledgment to the many authors whose publications have furnished the facts on which the story rests.